Once upon a time in
SIBERIA

Once upon a time in
SIBERIA

Harold Elvin

Anthony Blond

First published in Great Britain in 1985 by Anthony Blond.

Anthony Blond is an imprint of Muller, Blond & White Limited,
55 Great Ormond Street, London, WC1N 3HZ.

Copyright © 1985 Harold Elvin
British Library Cataloguing in Publication Data
Elvin, Harold
  Once upon a time in Siberia.
  I. Title
  823'.914[F] PR 6055.L/
  ISBN 0 856 34201 7

Typeset by D.P. Press Ltd, Sevenoaks, Kent.
Printed and bound in Great Britain by Billings and Son Ltd, Worcester

With great sadness, the publishers announce that Harold Elvin died before this book could be sent to press.

ACKNOWLEDGMENTS

TO
The Winston Churchill Memorial Trust, a Fellowship from whom enabled me to make an extensive journey through Siberia and Mongolia.

AND TO
Captain John Cochrane R.N.
Through Russian and Siberian Tartary – a Pedestrian Journey
John Murray, 1823

C.C. Coxwell
Siberian Tales
C.W. Daniel & Co. 1925

Jeremiah Curtin
Journey in Siberia
Samson, Lowe, Marston & Co., 1909

John Foster Fraser
The Real Siberia
D. Appleton & Co. 1902

Harmon Tupper
To the Great Ocean
Secker & Warburg, 1965

The Publishers would like to acknowledge the assistance of Christine Sutherland in providing the Afterword.

To Surya, my wife.

FOREWORD

The Americans crossed westwards to the Pacific. The Russians crossed eastwards to the Pacific.

The two movements met up in the north, in Alaska, which the Russians settled first, selling it in 1867 to the Americans for 7,200,000 dollars.

In each movement the spirit was that of migrants and settlers and not that of conquerors. The Czars named it 'peaceful penetration'.

The indigenous peoples of America, mainly Red Indians, gave some opposition to the American settlers. The indigenous peoples of Siberia and the surrounding eastern territories were always hospitable, welcoming, and willing to absorb all newcomers even including escaped convicts and Cossacks bent on imposing taxes. They were also never organised; living, at the best, in small disconnected communes. or, at the worst, in remote isolation.

Both migrations included those fleeing from religious persecution, criminals on the run, gold prospectors, bounty hunters, pioneers and masses looking for a new start in life. The Russians also included escaped serfs (there was never serfdom in Siberia), politicals and intellectuals escaping from the oppression of Czardom, prisoners-of-war from Sweden, Turkey, Poland, Bulgaria etc. and convicts despatched for a myriad of reasons.

Most of the land the Americans acquired was comparatively hospitable land. Most of the land the Russians acquired was inhospitable, especially in climate, and the weather killed as many convicts as did the harsh conditions the prisoners were forced to endure.

A high percentage of the convicts from Muscovy, and the prisoners-or-war too, having lived out their sentences, elected to stay on. The communes would grant them a plot of land, a cow and a horse and other first essentials, the ex-convicts would send for their wives, and the authorities, when the authorities came into the reckoning, would encourage them to stay. Because however intense the hells that the eastern countries held, Siberia nevertheless ever remained a haven for the free.

I

Zjennia was to marry Boris.

Boris was the he-man of the Samara country. Zjennia was the she-woman.

It was to be an explosion of a marriage.

As was the custom in their community, on the wedding night Zjennia knelt before Boris and touched one of his jack-boots. In one boot was to be a jewel, in the other a whip. If she chose the one with the jewel he must supply her with jewels and furs throughout their life. If she chose the one with the whip she should serve him, to the point of whipping, throughout their days.

She touched the one with the whip.

With a whoop that woke up hell he brandished the whip above her.

She touched the other boot and asked to see the jewel she had missed.

"Oh no!" he laughed. "You have had your choice."

Zjennia appealed to the priest, Alexis, who, also by custom, was present at this moment.

She appealed strongly, demanding the approval of the priest.

Feebly, Alexis concurred.

"Never!" shouted Boris and rushed to the door.

With a speed that lightning never equalled, she barred his way.

"I want to see the jewel," she said.

"I'll be back in a moment. I just have to leave the room for a minute."

She spread her arms across the door.

1

Then dived to his feet, wrenched at the second jack-boot and pulled out a second whip.

2

Zjennia gave Boris a night of glory, a saturnalia from the crucible of lust.

"Such men as you should taste, then waste," she said next day in her marshmallow voice. "I shall be master from now on."

3

Boris was caught stealing the emeralds from the St. Nikolai ikon in the town church and was sent in irons to the City of Samara.

He was sentenced "by order of the Czar" to serve out his natural span in Siberia.

Boris's friend, Stepan, was being dismissed from the jail the day that Boris was entering to await transportation. Stepan agreed to have horse and gun ready in the town if Boris could effect his escape during the coming evening.

Escaping more by strength than guile, Boris stood at ten at night outside the walls of the jail, by the Volga.

A figure so thin if it fell through a piccolo it'd have to try twice to make a note, approached.

"Follow me," it said.

"Where's Stepan?"

There was a ghoul of a shrug and the ghost moved off. Boris followed silently.

They walked to the heights above the Mother River and turned east down the Saratov Highway. A sudden gleaming on the golden domes of the Cathedral of the Lady of Kazan showed that a moon was about somewhere hiding behind the houses to the south.

Boris grabbed the flibbertigibbet and turned it fiercely towards him.

"Where's Stepan?"

Unmoved, the phantom shrugged just its shoulder.

"Did Stepan send you?"

A nod confirmed it.

"Where's the horse and the gun?"

"Follow me."

And the half of a shadow was off again.

The Church of Voznesenie was reached, then Czar Alexander Street. The roads became dirt and dust and no footways. The houses became shacks and, as if some power had pushed them back and back, the shacks faced each other across the street Volga-wide apart. Litters like barrels, like posts, like broken down hoardings, lay about forlorn as if left there by a by-gone age.

A sudden gap in the buildings and a slime of moon snaked across the road, dressing the pot-holes in eerie semen.

The two reached the outskirts.

The wraith turned right by some tumble-down fences and walked ten paces down. There was an animal with a gun across its saddle.

"This is not a horse. Where's the horse? What the hell. . ."

Boris swivelled round.

But the shades had reached out and snatched their brother back and swallowed it. Boris stood alone.

3

He stared back at the animal. It was not a horse, not even a pony, not even a cartoon of a horse. Tiny. Head drooping down. Donkeys drooped like that. Very tiny. There was a gun. There was a pig-skin made into a knapsack. Some packets of cartridges, a necessity or two, no food and no money.

Boris untethered this mockery of an animal and mounted.

The creature began running. It was not a trot, not a canter, simply running.

They were coming to the plank bridge that crossed a stream that led to the Samara River. A thousand times Boris had crossed it. But this time as the little running creature took him over he felt as if the bridge behind him was being heaved up like a portcullis with a wall rising on either side shutting off his return. A nightmare of unholiness stoppered him up inside and sat solid on his chest like a polyp.

He moved forward into the immensity of the east, into the miles and miles of miles and miles, into the dead ice-eye of moonlight.

A King was leaving his Kingdom.

Having learned that hell is only two steps outside paradise.

Leaving like a rat under the cover of night.

Only this King was not a rat.

4

Next evening Boris rode into Bulgucha, a small mining town.

He went to the inn and tethered his animal behind it by some waste-ground. At least a dozen horses stood in front but Boris saw that his would be a laughing-stock among them.

In the inn he said money was reaching him next day and, leaving his gun as security, took a room and food.

He slept twelve hours. One minute after awakening the black revisited him and, finding it too loaded a burden to bear, he tried to plunge back into sleep, but the sick horror in his memories forbade sleep.

Downstairs some miners were playing cards. He offered a jerkin he had found in his knapsack for a game. And lost.

He wandered out to the waste-ground behind the inn. On a low stone a stranger was squatting chewing straw. A stony face on a square of a man. The man kept on chewing and did not look up.

"I'll give you two hundred roubles for Poogavitsa*."

"Poogavitsa?"

The man chewed on and still did not raise his eyes.

"Your horse."

"Is that what it is?"

"Your horse. So."

"Loan?"

"Uh. For thirty-six hours. Thirty-six hours from now Poogavitsa will be given back to you in the condition he is now. Then you give me 100 roubles back. Then you can pay the inn, and what is left is yours. So."

The stranger seemed exhausted from his speech. He obviously never said twenty sentences if three would suffice.

Boris went to the fence, leaned on it, and thought.

"Why?" he asked.

Still neither man looked at each other.

*Poogavitsa: Russian for 'button'

5

"No whys. So." And the stranger chewed on.

Then he rose. Standing, he was a good height though squarely built, but beside the very tall Boris he looked short. Leaning by the gate by Boris, he said: "Two men recognised you last night. You'd do best to sleep in the barn at the end of this street this evening. Down the end. After the last house on the left. A hundred paces on. You'll find a barn. You'll be safe there. So." And he had the 200 roubles in his hand.

"And if you don't come back?" asked Boris.

"You'll have 200 roubles."

The size of the sum was baffling. A good horse was fifty roubles, a poor one, five. And he'd have his gun back. Boris took the money. But he might not take his horse back.

"At midnight tomorrow you'll have Poogavitsa. At the barn."

"Maybe," murmured Boris.

The stranger picked up a bag of oats and placed it over Poogavitsa's head. Boris saw some loose oats and tested them. He pressed one and the nourishment popped out. The oats were plump, heavy, succulent.

5

Bulgucha was filling up. Miners were obviously not working. The inn was crowded. Boris paid his bill and got his gun back.

"We'll have to push you to three to a room tonight," the innkeeper said.

"I'll not be staying."

The innkeeper looked at him in disbelief.

"Friends," muttered Boris. "Friends. . ."

He went out.

The crowd were leaving for outside town.

But Boris went to the barn. It was there as the stranger had said. And he laid down. The farm seemed strangely quiet.

As evening approached he mooched into town, but since the town had gone out-of-town, he followed a few stragglers all set in the same direction.

A noise reached him. Some cheering. Some jeering. A bedraggled motley mass was ringing an immense circle. Then a head appeared above the others, obviously in movement. On a horse! Then more. And a dozen, a score, were riding past unevenly. What manner of race was this? Then Poogavitsa! And the squat stranger upon it. Passing alone and to hoots of derision.

Boris had difficulty seeing the other side of the circle in the evening gloom. There was some board, and on it forty-two names, and there, at the bottom, Poogavitsa's name.

Boris asked: "How long does this continue?"

A man stared at him. "Are you a stranger, friend?"

"Yep. Sort of."

"It's the Bulgucha Festival. The 24-hour Endurance Stakes."

Horses were going at all conceivable speeds. It seemed a crazy affair. One rider dismounted, led his horse away, and went for a rest. Or for a wee. Fifteen minutes later he was back. One or two others did it. At the edge of the grotesque board with the names were the laps each had made. Poogavitsa had done 17. None other had done less than 22. And the derision of hoots stayed with the little button wherever it went.

The light failed and Boris could see the board no more. Presumably the race would go on all night. Beacons were being lit.

The stranger sat heavy on Poogavitsa. Now Boris could see: his horse ran as if being pulled invisibly by a string, there was no up and down movement: it looked as if his feet did not touch the ground, so perfect, so effortless was his running. And the stranger was immovable too. The pair seemed frozen together as one. Another lap had been lost and the derision each time the pair appeared increased.

Then the stranger raised himself slightly on his stirrups, took something from beneath the saddle and placed it in his mouth. Other pairs stopped for short or long spells, but not those two. This eased the lap score a little, but the pair was losing heavily.

Some bystanders thought the little titch should be removed from the arena but others answered "Later. Later."

Boris could no longer read the scoreboard; and wandered back to his barn.

Many of the crowd stayed all night.

At daybreak Boris returned. Poogavitsa was now 32 laps behind. The joke had gone too far and another move was being made to have the joker removed from the pack. But Boris noticed that only twenty horses were at that moment racing and he heard that five had dropped out altogether.

As the organisers made their move to check the course of Poogavitsa, the little horse passed two others and an ironical cheer went up from the spectators.

Then the stewards began disputing among themselves and one was knocked down. This caused much joy. "Never mind the steward. Was the horse hurt?" The betting had been furious and this horse was the favourite. Then everyone was arguing as to how t get their money back on the dying favourite – which was actually still running as if nothing had happened – and the crowd behaved like a boatload of monkeys ship-

8

wrecked in a storm. Then they spilled over, and over the official who had been kicked unconscious on the skull.

Three horses decided to discontinue whatever their riders might do. And a rest they had made no difference, they still refused to budge. A man put his hand on Boris's arm: "You can't blame them. All that bloody effort and what do they get out of it? It's the lazy bum on top what gets the loot."

The favourite withdrew but word got buzzed around that he'd be back in an hour.

Again the rider raised himself on Poogavitsa's back and removed more food from under the saddle and bunged it into his mouth. "The bugger hasn't even stopped to pee yet," said the man, still with his hand on Boris's arm. "Don't you believe it. He's pee'd all over the course," said his neighbour.

"And crapped too."

The horses left running by noon were down to 21 and Poogavitsa's deficiency was down to 24 laps. The derisions grew less.

Some riders failed. Some horses failed. Some burst into spasmodic gallops. Some died to a canter. Some to a walk. Poogavitsa ran on.

No one had bet on the little one. But cheers that were now only half derisory were coming its way.

The birches and larches stood sentinel. The open sky looked down. Two thousand souls of rags and bones, of string and paper and fish-skin shoes, of torn kafkans and schubas,* of Russians, Buriats, Tungusis, Turks, gypsies and Finns, all embroiled in this curiosity called "The Race of the Century" "The World's Endurance Stakes" "The Horse of the Universe".

Only two hours to go and only twelve horses left.

*Schubas: Russian version of fur and skin coats

9

Poogavitsa was fifteen laps behind.

Most horses struggled. Most were resting more and more.

Half an hour to go and the incredible happened: the stranger aboard Poogavitsa touched the flanks of his charger and their speed doubled.

Now the packed arena gaped. The rider had not dismounted once and the horse not slackened pace for a moment: the rider still fed himself mouthful by mouthful from underneath the saddle. Rumour went round that he had raw meat there and the heat of his body had cooked it.

That the speed of Poogavitsa was doubled was obvious. Yet not obvious. That action, that apparent lack of effort was the same. The little one began to run past the others as if someone was pulling the invisible string at double the speed.

Five horses now were left only, and the incongruous pair were only three laps behind.

It was into the realms of disbelief and is still talked about in Bulgucha till this day: the little one 'walked it', except, as all could see, it 'ran it'.

Then, as it *lapped* the last horse, the arena cheered and screamed and stampeded and there are some who say that the race never got finished.

Others say that Poogavitsa is running there still.

6

In spite of all that, Boris still did not want Poogavitsa back and decided to strike a bargain *if* the stranger returned.

At midnight there was the sound of hooves. The stranger was astride a splendid mount and the wan little Poogavitsa was beside him.

"My name is Sergei. Shall we go?"

"Go?"

They were to ride out together? In a daze, not wanting to leave, Boris nevertheless brought his gun and knapsack out, mounted his midget and they all rode off.

They rode in silence.

It was into daylight when they reached a river. Perhaps it was only fifty paces wide but it was impossible to cross.

Sergei turned right and down a small winding track.

After a hundred paces the track died at the river's edge. Across the river on the opposite bank was a raft.

"Give us a hand," Sergei said. And it was the first sentence spoken in all that time.

Boris went with him to the water's edge. Just out of sight, because of the abnormal height of the reeds, was a double-wheel contraption at head height. There was a rope from this to the opposite bank. Then Boris realised there were two ropes. Then he realised there was another double-wheel on the opposite bank and the raft could be pulled back and forth from side to side. The current was strong but slowly the raft came over. They mounted with their horses and the two men pulled the raft back across the river.

They made a fire and had tea and black bread.

'Well,' thought Boris, 'I might as well do it.' And he took out the hundred roubles he owed. But he still decided to sell Poogavitsa further on.

Sergei took the money, added another hundred, and offered it back.

"What's this?"

Sergei rolled his lips in a spit. "Take it!" he said.

"What for?"

11

"Take it, man! Bury your bloody pride!"

"I don't want it."

"Then give it to bloody Poogavitsa! He won it, didn't he? Buy him some decent oats. And a bottle of vodka too if he'll accept it. Here it is, in your knapsack. Chuck it out if you like. But don't offer it to me! So!"

And he was moving to mount his horse.

Boris said: "Did you win much?"

"Thousand."

And Sergei was on his way.

No one spoke to Boris like that. And here was an imposter of a companion. . . Boris would not only part with Poogavitsa soon, but with Sergei too.

Boris was a leader. He had been as a boy, and he had been as a man. He was sometimes a chosen leader, and sometimes a self-chosen leader. But he led. Strongly. And never rudely. And by some mysterious quirk, no one was ever rude to him. He lived in a rough world where men, and women too, spent half their time abusing each other. And answering back. Yet, for no fathomable reason, no one was ever sarcastic to him: strongly spoken, firm perhaps, differing often: but never with that element of abuse they kept for everyone else. And never curt, like this stranger.

Boris lived by his nature, without reasoning it. His father had been sarcastic once and the relationship had never been the same again. His father had often been harsh, authoritarian: Boris accepted that. But abuse or sarcasm against his self riled him, and the father had never been able to regain that relationship that had been before that sarcastic burst.

So Boris, so quickly, had had enough of Sergei.

"The Urals," Sergei motioned in front of him.

Yes, there were the Urals. Europe ended there and Asia began. Russia closed its doors there and Siberia opened its giant's yawn.

12

A boundary made by geography and confirmed by history.

7

They crossed the Ural heights by Knievka and began their descent.

They turned from the highway to a byway and rested there among the aspens and the larches.

A sound of shouting reached them and then of a grinding of wheels over the surface. A coach loomed – the post waggon. By a freak in the dip of the high road they saw the coach first and the horses later. First two horses, then four appeared, and by then the coach itself was lost to view.

A shot rent the air and a horseman flashed down upon the carriage. Amidst the pandemonium and the slithering of the horses and the realisation of the hold-up, there was a double panic.

The passengers were arraigned outside and the drivers too. The hooded horseman shouted at them.

He was handed two leather-bags – small pig's-skins sewn up, fastened with heavy steel chains and locked. He despatched a bullet to heaven and was off.

A passenger and a coachman drew guns, the rider's horse stumbled and fell and the bean-pole of a robber dropped the bags and ran with more shots raging.

"Quick!" shouted Boris. "I'll save the rider. You save the loot."

And he had gone.

He was soon beside the horseman now running for his life, shouted to him to spring up behind, and the two

13

were away and back to the tiny track and into the shelter of the woodlands.

Yes, and Sergei had followed and had the bags: one heavy, one light, one with money, one with mail. Each padlocked with the seal of Czar Peter the Great's Postal Service.

8

The lone horseman was so tall that on his way to the sky he had hit a cloud which had bent him over like a bent pin at his shoulders.

But just now he was at one moment bowed like a weeping willow, at the next jumping about like corn in a shovel: he was a rag-bag of characters and none of them savoury.

"I acted on impulse," Boris said as he went over to him as their fire was dying at their bivouac that evening. "You were cornered and I can't stand seeing a man cornered. Here are your bags. Be off between dawn and sunrise. You'll be safe with us for the night. Your life is your own. Take it with you. Your winnings are your own. Take them also. I haven't seen you and you haven't seen me."

As if the sun broke through the clouds across a meadow, gangleshanks showed relief across his face, then said: "My name is Viktor. I've lost my horse."

"Malvolets is twenty miles to the north and Ufa only seventy. Buy yourself a stable of horses. Don't be here at sunrise. That's an order." And he was leaving.

The horseman called him back. "And Sergei?"

"Sergei can do what he damn well likes."

14

"I've told him I'd pay him."

"Pay him! Take him off too if he wants to go. Just don't offer me a kopeck. I'll speak with him. If he goes with you, he goes with you. If he stays with me and has one coin upon him, then the three of us will go three different ways."

9

Next morning Boris thought he was alone. But Sergei was on the horizon staring down at the valley.

Boris went slowly to him.

"You are still here?"

Sergei gave a yes-shake of his head.

"Have you a kopeck of his money?"

Sergei shook his head in the negative.

"Why? Why have you stayed with me?"

Sergei rested his hand on Boris's shoulder. Boris wanted to brush it off, but listened.

Sergei said: "As one bollock said to the other bollock: why should we hang? It's that thin fellow out in front what did the shooting."

10

"Why did you join me at Bulgucha?" asked Boris.

"You are a fair man. So."

"How do you know I am a fair man?"

"I smell it. Unfair men stink. So."

"I am not an honest man."

Sergei spat. "Who asked for honesty? Honesty and dishonesty are games. If you tell the first militiaman we meet I helped rob that coach, that might be honest, but it would get you no mark in heaven. Hide me from that militiaman, though you know I had done a thousand crimes, and there's pith in that. Uh. So. Honesty and dishonesty are diseases of the tongue. A fair man is above all that."

"Why do you want a companion at all?"

"So. You must be new here. There are three things you must know. Firstly, brodyagi: escaped convicts and criminals, petty and mighty who hunt in packs. They are starving, and desperate, and willing to kill any lone man for his boots. With two of you, you have a chance. Four is better. Six is best. Secondly, Cossacks. They also are in packs. They say of two evils, the least is a good. Then settle for the Cossacks as the good. They are devils, tax collectors, brigands but with their own sense of right. Wild. I like them. But they are a scourge, conquering under the pretext of doing it in the holy name of the Czar. Thirdly, the biggest scourge of all. The winter. Eight months of it. And it can kill. So. More than all the scourges. I like that too. It's fierce. But fair – like you. With two, or four, or six, there can be hope to survive."

"I don't know what you are running away from. I see no brand upon you. Perhaps you escaped before you were branded. Perhaps you are fleeing for a private reason. I will tell you this. Put a thousand miles between you and the place you left and the world is yours. . . except for the place you left. Neither brodyagi, Cossack or Siberian peasant will hold anything against you, your life is your own. Only that the All Mighty Czar of all the Russias has locked your front door back home and sent

16

you out to count the birches."

"Why did you choose Poogavitsa for your race?"

"Uh!" Sergei raised his hand and palmed it down, he didn't want to rant on. Talking was an exhausting matter.

They turned to leave their camp.

Sergei mounted, and set off.

Boris cried out: "Sergei! Listen. Come back a moment."

Sergei returned.

"Be quiet and listen."

Just as both had decided there was nothing, a distant groan reached them.

"Did you hear?"

Sergei nodded.

Boris shouted loudly: "Whoever you are, wherever you are, keep on groaning. We'll find you."

Another long pause. It seemed impossible.

Again as they were mounting to leave, again the groan.

"Once more! Once more!" shouted Boris.

And both set off searching.

Only thirty paces away, Boris saw a boot. He went to it, raised the fern and brushwood, and there was a man thin as a corpse, cheeks so indrawn as to touch each other inside, eyes with death sitting on them. Yet staring still.

And on both wrists, manacles.

II

Boris moistened the man's lips, then held the head up and forced a little water down.

"I'm staying," said Boris.

He expected Sergei to answer but Sergei shrugged instead, which looked as if it was an acceptance that he'd stay too.

Then Sergei grew restless and said: "I'm off on a hunt. I've seen fox and rabbit marks. So."

For hours there was little to do, but then the man murmured something. Boris could not understand. Then Boris understood that the man was Georgian.

It was after two days of slow revival that it registered on the man that he could not be understood. This nettled him, then Boris asked: "Georgian?"

"Yes."

"We, Russian."

"You, Russian?"

"Yes."

The man spoke a little Russian and asked for more water and tried a smile when he received it, then bread, and he attempted another smile.

Sergei, who went off for long periods returning with a hare, a pheasant once, a brace of partridges once, said: "Boris, this Georgian will need a month to be fit."

"I'll stay a week," said Boris, "then decide."

A sigh and a nod from Sergei, and he had mounted his horse again. "We are only five miles from Verkneuralsk," he said, and rode off.

After five days Boris turned Shermadin, the Georgian,

18

over on his front, stretched the manacled hands above the head, and raised his gun. Horrified, Sergei saw too late, and a shot rang out.

The manacles split in two.

Still staring, relieved but shattered, Sergei stared on.

The shock of the shot alone could have killed the Georgian.

Boris went across, gently turned Shermadin over, rested his back against a tree trunk, and said "Look, two hands again." And he held up one hand, and then the other.

The man only stared at Boris. Stared and stared. Boris had expected an immediate joy. "This will help you. Look, your hands are free."

Sergei came and stood over. He was puzzled but made no comment. Boris had expected Sergei to praise his action also. But Sergei didn't.

Then Shermadin lifted one hand independent of the other and watched it go up. And then down. And then the other hand. It was something beyond his grasp. Still Boris awaited a smile: a hint of joy.

Boris had been manacled for one hour only in Samara. He had felt stripped of all dignity, and dignity was what Boris had a mountain of. No man must be manacled! Ever. Let no man ever be manacled in this world again!

Once more Shermadin raised a left hand. Up, he watched it. Down, he watched it. Then the right hand.

"See," said Boris. "Sergei, I have freed him."

Still Sergei said nothing, and Boris was bewildered, with a nugget of anger.

And Boris played with the man's hands, up, down, up, down. "He has been manacled for seven years!" said Boris.

12

Sergei went far away that day and returned with some perch. While away Shermadin asked Boris: "How did you pick up with that fellow?"

"Sergei? I didn't pick him up. He picked me up."

"Last time I saw him, there were six of them."

"You know him?"

"No. I saw him. He never saw me. Where are the other five?" Later he mumbled: "Mystery."

That evening Sergei went over to Shermadin and had a long conversation with him — long by Sergei's standards.

Returning, Sergei said, "Tomorrow I'll ride into Verkneuralsk."

"Why?"

"To find a blacksmith."

"Will there be one?"

This is an iron mining area and every village has a blacksmith. Come to think of it, perhaps every village in Siberia has a blacksmith. There used to be 5 million horses in Siberia."

"And now?"

"Four million."

"Why the difference?"

Sergei sat as if he was actually going to start a conversation.

"In 1857 an English engineer called Mr. Dull came this way and estimated five million horses in Siberia of which a million died every year from winter or from hunger. But he saw how the horses pulled the trucks on

20

railways lines at the mines so proposed to Czar Alexander the building of a horse tramway to the Pacific with five changes of horses a day. The Czar loved the idea and sought for tenders but none were forthcoming. Dull thought it would have saved the dying horses but all it did was to give birth to the Trans-Siberian Railway Dream. Dull repeated the offer to build it himself in 1860 if he could have Russian support, but again he gained no encouragement beyond the Czar's."

Sergei rose. No doubt feeling he had fulfilled his quota of talking for the day.

13

The seven days were up and gone and no one had discussed departure. It had been accepted without discussion that when Shermadin could be moved, he would ride behind Sergei on Sergei's mount Kukurooza* to visit the blacksmith. "What I began, you will finish," said Boris.

Sergei looked puzzled.

"With the manacles. . ." added Boris.

"Mm."

He still awaited a word from Shermadin or from Sergei about his shooting. He thought he had done well.

But Sergei had a different surprise. "I bought two revolvers," he said. "We had better have instant protection." And he handed one to Boris.

"I'll pay you later," and Boris accepted the gift.

Sergei made one of his spitting shrugs of the shoulder.

*Kukurooza: Russian for 'maize, Indian corn'

21

14

It was on the tenth day that Shermadin was to make his effort.

He was lifted up behind Sergei, then strapped to him so that he could not fall off. Boris was proud to see how, with all that weakness, it helped him to have free hands.

Boris rode behind.

They were early at the forge, but already the town was astir.

"There's a trial on today," said the blacksmith. "They've caught that Great Post robber and they'll be hanging him tonight."

The Elders had decided that they would hold the trial among themselves. Even the hint of an official judge from Ufa or Cheliabinsk would lessen the fame that should be Verkneuralsk's alone and by unanimous decision it was decreed that they could not hold such a criminal to await a judge, as the dangerous outlaw band, the fiercest in Siberia, of which he was but one, would burn the whole town to the ground to effect his release, so the only course open was to proceed instantly.

All Verkneuralsk was agog and half descended on the courts, which were not courts but the commune town hall, which was not a commune town hall, but a school hall, which was not a school hall but a large space in the Chief Elder's grounds where occasionally someone taught the Chief Elder's illegitimate Buriat children Russian, which lesson was always replaced by the Cossack craft of how to stick a pig.

Boris and Sergei, having deposited Shermadin with

the blacksmith, managed to squeeze in to the hall. All people awaited the presence of the 'most wanted man since Yermak'.

There were women there, expected to swoon away at the sight of such a one. Most men had beards, and all women bright shawls covering their heads.

There was a rough long trestle table and some stools, while a servant proudly, though blushing in hang-dog style, came and set down a typewriter which, if they had had typewriters in the 10th century would have been the first of even them. No one present could type, but it lent tone to display that there was an instrument in town. An abacus came next. Everyone could use that because no one ever counted in any other way. There was no use for the abacus, but that too lent tone.

The criminal was about to be brought in. Such a stir was in the wood-beamed room that the rafters shook with the increased pulse rate. Half thought they should jeer, half, in their depths, wanted to cheer. But when the bent bean-pole entered between two shy stooping guards the pulse dropped from over to under normal and the women felt cheated.

Boris and Sergei touched arms: yes! it was their man, the redoubtable Viktor.

Boris wanted to rush away before they were recognised but remained glued. Sergei's pressure on his arm acted to help rivet him to his stool.

The Elders came. They expected a cheer but never got it. They also had beards, and it was in their beards that they held distinction. The Apostles never had such nobility in beardliness as these five: the one and only priest; the one and only schoolmaster (who taught pig-sticking instead of Russian); Nikodimov, who owned a tallow factory and employed half the town; Borodin, who owned the only saloon and managed to regain most of the money Nikodimov paid out; and Zurnikov, who owned this outsized parlour, sometime school, sometime town hall, now a court of law. He was the Chief Elder and his were most of the decisions. He also had the finest beard – the only pointed Don Quixotian one in town.

The Great Coach robber stood there forested around with fetters. He was billed as Verkneuralsk's most daring outlaw since Pugachev. Viktor drooped like a lank, dank lily, his expression looked as crooked as a snake with colic, and Pugachev would have risen again if that was all they could find for comparison.

The chief witness was brought in, and he at last got a cheer. A dapper man with a cane from Birsk twelve miles away. An anachronism in a rural setting: over his shoulders he wore a cloak and no coat, such as actors did at times; a hat almost like a bowler, a pair of thin wired spectacles in vogue in St. Petersburg, but never before seen here in Verkneuralsk. His apparel was the beginning and the end of all that was dignified about him.

He told his story in a falsetto voice making him even less rural than ever.

Such a fear had swept that hillock in the Urals that the appeals of the passengers would haunt the mountain passes forever, and hover like a death-mist always in those valleys, while one man's fearlessness (his own) had stood out and he had drawn his pistol and stilled the horse that grounded the horseman (except that it had been the coachman's shot which had hit).

He (the fearless one) recognised the highwayman, Lavrenti Nakhimov, ill-famed descendant of Russia's most-famed Admiral – so Viktor was now Lavrenti Nakhimov? – when passing through this noble town – the awe-stricken crowd liked that, and the 'actor' noted that they liked it, and should give them more of it, but what could one say about such a god-forsaken,

24

flea-bitten, rat-infested dump where not even the Chief Elder had any worthy jack-boots to his name? He recognised the highwayman in the saloon because of his second coat sticking out from under his top-coat and because of his daring who-cares look. (Boris had never seen a shiftier, more mouse-like giraffe than the prisoner was portraying at that moment.) He (the great one) befriended the prisoner and after getting him drunk accompanied him to his room where the loot was hidden with the post-locks on it, and, and. . .

The Elders felt a need for refreshment and therefore announced that the court would resume 'saychas'. 'Saychas' in Russian means 'immediately', in translation it means 'in an hour', which sometimes means 'in a day', at other times, 'in a month', after which further 'saychas's' can be repeated until everyone has forgotten why the first saychas cropped up. Or as in Spanish 'mañana' means 'tomorrow' but most look upon it as meaning 'never'. While in Hindi 'kol' can mean either 'tomorrow' or 'yesterday'. Which all might help prove the point that existence is one long protracted 'now'.

Since 'saychas' once in a hundred years means 'saychas', the crowd decided to sit it out and it was found that most had come prepared with beer, doughnuts and gingerbread. The courtroom therefore became a jolly place.

15

After a three-hour 'immediately' and much vodka the Elders returned to the court, their prisoner with them overloaded with fetters, like a

Christmas tree in chains. Some jeered him. None cheered him.

Zornikov, as Chief Elder, spoke. "One of the gweatest quimes in history has been wesolved this day. Verkneuralsk will be a m-marked place for years to come. C-common quiminals will fear this p-place. Hiccough. One of the most clever highwaymen of all time will be meted out his justice this day and his accomplices sought throughout the whole length and breadth of the land. Their names will be issued, their descwiptions issued and they will be sought from the Pacific to the Atlantic. Hiccough. I have been asked to deliver the sentence.

"That th-this most dangerous qweature standing before you shall be responsible for the gilding of the dome of our gweat church. That this he does as token to the God in the H-Highest to appease for his tewwible quime.

"That also, the aforementioned scoundwel standing before you shall be wesponsible for the enlargement of this school by an additional woom so that all childwen shall have the benefit of the Czar's gweat education pwogramme.

"Thirdly, that this villain, here that you see chained, captured alive in our town shall pay from his own purse for one hundred candles to be in constant burning throughout each Sabbath in the coming year, such candles to be purchased from our gweat factory the Nikodimov Tallow and Scandal C-company.

"Fourthly" – and here the great Elder paused to take a sip from a metal container inside his balloon shirt – "this self-confessed villain shall pay our gweat witness hiccough of our gweat neighbour commune Birsk, the sum due to him as reward for apprehending the villain, to which we all in our gweat town of Verkneuralsk would add our thanks and pwaise for

26

courage and perspic- perspic . . . per . . . per . . . per. . . thwoughout.

"Fifthly, that the aforemen-mentioned quiminal here chained before you shall pwesent to the town the finest horsehide jack-boots to be purchased at the Fair of Tobolsk for pwesentation to the Chief Elder of this c-commune, these boots to be passed on in perpet. . . perpetu. . . per. . .

"Sixthly, shall all those among you who so wishes, when this session of this Court closes, repair in a quiet and orderly manner to the saloon of our fine elder, Borodin, to dwink to this day when justice has been done: the aforementioned dwinks to be paid for in full by the aforementioned villain. . ."

Riotous applause.

"Finally, Kropotkin our pwoud blacksmith, no finer in the Empire of the Czars". . . applause for everything now . . . "Kropotkin will unseal the pig-skin bag before us all so that you can all bear witness to our utter, utterly, utterly honesty, and he will release it from its Postal Seal.

"Finally, our gweat quimminal, hiccough, here before you, has agreed to allev. . . allevi. . . his quime and wemorse to name the twue villains of this robbery, to name those who planned and forced him against his will to carry it thwough. . ."

Boos.

"He will now name these villains, hiccough, for whom hell is too sweet a place. . . and for each quiminal name he shall himself receive 100 roubles for his couwage from the gwateful Czar of all the Russias and the nation. . ."

Boris had his hand on his revolver: he wouldn't get those names out: Sergei held his hand on Boris's arm. . .

No one heard the names.

"Speak louder, prisoner!"

27

Boris still kept his hand on his holster. . .

Five Buriat names came out.

Boris released his grasp.

"And 500 roubles to Viktor," winked Sergei. "For five non existing Buriats."

The bag was brought in.

"One bag?" asked Boris.

"One bag. So," winked Sergei.

After a great display of professional expertise their friend Kropotkin, the good blacksmith, forced the seal and the lock on the pig-skin bag. Letters and documents tumbled out.

But to prove the honesty of the Elders and the good citizens of Verkneuralsk, all letters and documents would be returned to the Post with their seals untouched.

Integrity was the watchword in Verkneuralsk.

16

At the blacksmith's forge Boris noticed, flung into a corner, the second Post pig-skin bag unlocked and empty. He pointed it out to Sergei who nodded his usual 'Yes. Of course.' There was a silver rouble left at the bottom.

"What do you think, just one? The Courts will forgive me?" And Boris put it in his pocket.

"Just one," Sergei winked his yes again.

Then they joined the orderly crowd to the saloon. Only it was a stampede.

A cheery, happy stampede. Each man satisfied that justice had not only been done but was about to be seen to be done.

At some time that evening Viktor, now Lavrenti, appeared. No chains. With a buzz in his ear like gnats. Only that the gnats were Verkneuralskis attacking him with glory. He now looked, what he was, a long proliferation, half-gangle and half-shanks. Now sword-sharp, as busy giving out drinks as a bear being attacked by a beehive. Then, suddenly he turned, and there was a brick wall before him. That brick wall was Boris and Sergei.

". . .moment!" And Viktor had vanished.

In a flash he was back with two bottles. He pressed one each into the hands of the two friends. The best vodka.

Viktor looked firmly-shiftly at them, a look that perhaps only he could perfect.

"I can always recognise a face that I have never seen before!" he said.

"Never seen before," the pair repeated.

"That's a funny thing," pressed on Viktor, "I just always *could* recognise a face that I. . ."

". . .have never seen before!" they all three repeated together.

No one knew that night in which direction Verkneuralsk was going. Everyone had different opinions about it. Many got lost trying to prove the other wrong.

The man with the cane from Birsk met Boris and Sergei in the street and said: ". . .'strordinary thing, I could swear, swear that other side of the road was over there. D'you know – secret! – over there they told me it was over here!"

The priest stood a long time staring up at the only street lamp in Verkneuralsk: "There are no limits to the miracles of the Lord: behold, the sun is shining in the dark!"

17

The Vesuvius inside Zjennia had begun once more signalling its happy havoc around Samara province.

Her unctious skin, her laugh like sunshine, the svelteness of her touch, her imperial power hidden in her marshmallow voice, her torrid soul, her needle of fire in her hazel green eye, her voluptuous breasts like bowls of cream uncurdled, her wobble wasp in her coiling walk. . .

As she walked down her laughter-lane to visit Alexis, the priest, grandpapa threw away his crutches and did a jig, children jockeyed for position to be kissed, boys found they were men, and women decided to send their menfolk along 'to learn'.

The Mother River burst its banks to get near her.

"Alexis," she said, "my elder sister, Eva, has a great trouble. She is engaged to Popovitch the wealthiest tea merchant in Samara, but she has developed a great detestation for him, as well as developing a deep passion for Nikolai our popular schoolmaster. How can Eva get out of it?"

"Uterus teeth."

"What do you mean by uterus teeth? And why are you sitting at the other end of the room?"

"Because if I come closer, Yevgennia Dimitrovna, I would drool rather than talk and you are asking me a thinking question."

"Then hurry up with your answer! Then be sensible and come closer and drool."

"Uterus teeth saved one virgin I knew. And we have to save Eva, because the drawback in marrying a person for his wealth is that you then have to live with him. You announce that the unfortunate Eva has developed a rare malady called uterus teeth and any knight who ventures inside has his pride hospitalised – for life."

"Oh I like that," cackled Zjennia "but they'll insist upon an examination."

"Exactly, my dear orchid – you see I'm drooling already though I am an ocean distant away. Leave that to me. And to the doctor, of course. We'll have Eva fitted up with a dried cod's head in her womb, and the teeth will gleam threateningly frighteningly back at any who get a glance therein. It cannot fail."

"Alexis, you are such a wonderful saviour. I will put it to Eva. Why have you never been near me, Alexis? Are you aiming to be the last man in town?"

"I have been near you, Zjennia. I am with you every night. Perhaps I was the first, and I'll certainly be the last." He was blushing like a virgin in Hell.

"Alexis, are you a bad man?"

"Priests have to find their own answers."

"But you were the stallion of the north. What was it that happened in that village near Malmis?"

"It was the law there and the Church sanctioned it."

"That you slept with every woman?"

"That I deflowered every virgin the night before her wedding. So that I could declare to society that she had been virgin."

"How many virgins?"

"The entire neighbourhood."

"And you keep from me? And enjoy me every night? Oh sweet Alexis, what evil naughtiness is in this?"

"You fill my imagination from cry of dawn till croak of day. And by night you fill my bed – my imagined bed."

"Then, you wicked man, you owe this woman before you, a fortune! What price per night would I fetch in the markets of Samara City? Ten silver roubles?"

"A hundred. Ten thousand if I were the judge."

"Then, priest, not prince, do your sums, how many times have you enjoyed me in your imaginings? There are 365 days in the year – or do you exclude Sundays?"

"Sundays, twice. Once for the glory of the Lord who made you."

"Then multiply by how many years, and honour your debts. Do I deserve less than a common courtesan?"

"You deserve the crown of a. . . of a. . ." and he whispered almost inaudibly "goddess."

"Alexis! I want my money! And you are not even drooling yet."

"If I drooled," he was looking down at the carpet, "it would be awful, not noble."

"Then pay up else I'll take you to court."

"There'd be no need." He still looked down.

"Why not?"

"You would win. Court case, and all."

"Then? Priest Alexis?"

"The court would decide the whole debt. In your favour."

"Then?"

"Then." He seemed to concentrate on looking down, at one spot. "The court would decide that just as my actions had been imaginings, so should the payments be, and an imaginary coffer of gold should be waved back and forth in front of your imagination."

"Alexis! Come here!"

He went.

She hit him hard across the cheek. Many men liked that. And Alexis would too – in his imaginings.

"You are the biggest cheat in Muscovy!" she half screamed and half laughed. "And in the Church too!"

32

"No. The Church would understand. Because otherwise I would have had to rob the Church to pay you. And all the churches have not enough in all of Muscovy for your deserts. And worse, they might have sent me away." An odd half smile and half sigh crept into his face.

"Don't smile at cheating me! Now, priest, instead of my being down on my knees in front of you, you, priest, go down on your knees in front of me!"

He did so.

"Alexis, I feel I've got uterus teeth coming on. And I'm in search of a knight to destroy. My hot-house flower is going to bite off your ramrod every night for a week. If you don't satisfy me I will expose your felonies to the wide world – and with the addition of my imaginings. But for tonight, it has to be instant. Then for the other six nights I want this room with flowers and candles and a couch bestrewn with great hides and satinned cushions. Justice is jealous for revenge. Begin to pay your debts in kind! Or else. . ."

18

Boris and Sergei slept in the blacksmith's forge. Shermadin was there beside them on the hay.

They were preparing to leave when Boris, aghast with horror, saw that Shermadin had been manacled again.

"He was to be freed at the wrists!"

The blacksmith who had come forward nodded "No."

Sergei nodded "No."

"What the hell!!. . ." And Boris rushed to Shermadin.

"Is this right? Don't be afraid to tell me! I will put it right! Don't be afraid!"

"It is right," murmured Shermadin. But it was only a whisper, and Boris paced about. Then again he went to Shermadin.

"Don't be afraid, I tell you! I will put it right!"

"It is right."

"So I have saved your life, that you shall lose it again?"

Sergei came forward. "You have saved his life, that his wife and children shall live. If we can get him back to his prison-camp the way he left it and before the Cossacks make their inspection, it is best. All will be well. If he is not there, the Cossacks will kill his wife and children."

"Your wife and children live with you?"

Boris did not want to talk with Sergei. He only wanted to hear words from Shermadin.

"Yes."

"In the camp?"

"Yes."

"As prisoners?"

"Yes."

"And they will be killed if you do not go back?"

"Yes."

Boris felt a split in his head: a sick head-ache. He turned to Sergei: "How far is the camp?"

"We can make it in two days. The Cossacks come twice a year."

"Why?"

"For their taxes."

"And they count the numbers?"

"Yes. So."

"And if one is missing?"

"His family are killed."

"Why?"

34

"The Cossacks get an allowance from the Czar per head of household. And they don't reckon on losing their subsidy."

"We will be in time?"

"Yes, in time. Shermadin will ride in front of me now. We will go gently. His family will nurse him back to health. Also the whole community is fined if one is missing."

But they didn't reckon with Poogavitsa! He had no version of riding gently. He ran: and that was all.

"Keep the reins gently pulled in. It will slow him a little. He will obey. But he will not understand," said Sergei.

And Boris tried that and it helped. But it was an awkward ride. Poogavitsa was always ahead and had constantly to be halted.

At one stop Boris went over to Shermadin: "Why did you escape?"

"I have an illness."

"What is your illness?"

"No one understands."

"But what is it?"

Shermadin went on: "I become ill if I live for years on the flat. No one knows of this illness. I have not heard of it before, have you?"

"No."

"I have heard a few Georgians mention it. You see, in Georgia we have mountains. And this prison-camp is in vast areas of flat terrain. It's physical: I mean, the sickness. A year was all right. After three years it became unbearable. After seven years I could support it no longer and had to get out. I did reach the mountains, didn't I?"

Sergei passed tea to Boris and looked Boris in the eyes, and Boris understood.

"Well," said Boris. "Very high hills, we must say that at the least."

"Nearly mountains?"

"Oh yes."

"The Urals," said Sergei.

"Yes, the Urals," said Boris.

"To get up that last climb took it out of me. I knew it was a mountain. No wonder I collapsed."

It had been a mere hillock, a pimple. "A great mountain," said Boris.

"I never meant to leave my people," said Shermadin. "I meant to return. After two or three days in the mountains. And I actually had more than a week, didn't I? Didn't I?"

"Yes, more than a week."

"Fine air it was," said Sergei. "Thin air."

"Yes, thin air. I can't explain. It's a physical thing you know," persisted Shermadin. "Can't explain that to a judge, can you? They don't realise, do they, in the courts, that the same sentence for different men means different sentences. Did you ever ask yourself what happens to a condemned man with claustrophobia? We had one man who must have ten hours sleep a night else he went mad. They wouldn't let him. He went mad. They didn't understand. I didn't mean to stay away, you know. I meant just to reach the mountains then return."

"What are you in prison for?"

"Opponent of the Czar."

Sergei intervened. "They have no need to ask. In Georgia every man, woman and child is an opponent of the Czar. You can sentence any one of them, and it will be a right sentence. Shermadin probably did nothing. We should go."

"One more question," asked Boris. "How long more have you to serve?"

"Five years. If I can last it, we can all go home then, and the little ones too. To Georgia. By train!" And there came a little smile and there came a little hope.

36

19

They were approaching the prison camp. The outskirts looked as if a tornado had blasted them. Buildings were akimbo. Deserted, wrecked, scattered.

But inside looked orderly. A very long street of single houses. An open prison? A few children were making signs that they recognised Shermadin, and they started dashing about.

Into the centre the motley trio rode.

The whole camp was in manacles!

20

The odd assorted trio, on the tallest and shortest horses the village had ever seen, rode into the prison camp and stopped at the centre house.

The elders of the prison commune came out to meet them. In manacles.

It was Sergei who spoke: "Your friend Shermadin was on his way back here and we expedited his return by offering him a piggy-back. He has suffered an ordeal and is weak and although you will want to interview him perhaps you could send word to his wife and children?" Sergei breathed heavily out. Such a long speech was always exhausting.

The elders took all three in and immediately tea was brought to them. It was a log cabin with a heavy deal table and stools. There were no furnishings but the airy room was clean.

Shermadin was put into a side room.

Cabbage soup was brought with much cabbage floating in it.

"He was far from here?" asked one. These elders also all had beards. And one at least had dignity. The manacles lent a bizarre dimension to the scene. Boris felt sick in a horror.

"Why is the village in manacles?" asked Boris.

"One minute," interposed Sergei, "Shermadin was four days' walk from here, down the west road. We brought him here in two days. But, as you see, he is weak. Continue, Boris. . ." Then added to the elders, "My friend Boris is new to Siberia."

"We are in manacles," spoke the first elder, "by courtesy of the Cossacks."

"By courtesy of?"

"We are considered brigands of the highest order. We work in a boot factory sixteen hours a day. We three here only are free from the factory. We – all the camp – lived in the prison block that you saw destroyed as you entered here. We now work in the factory you will pass on your way as you leave. Every morning at 5.0 a.m. even through sleet or blizzard or 40 degrees below zero, we used to be marched the length of this street to our work. We are forever manacled. Then we made a splendid deal with the Cossacks. They allowed us the freedom to build ourselves homes. Most prisoners share. A few have sent for their wives and families. But the shackles remain. For the wives too and for all children over twelve. A few children have been born here and, in their minds, the world is shackled. If a prisoner dies we must keep his body till the Cossacks see it with their own eyes. We three elders are chiefly responsible to see that all laws are kept. If Shermadin had not returned one of the three of us would have been used as target practice. The Cossacks like that. It's sport, they say. And also each man in the camp would have been fined. . . with cut rations as well. The Cossacks will not come for four weeks and we will get Shermadin working again and his manacle chain the right colour."

Yes, it did look too new, Boris had noticed that.

"What awful men are these Cossacks."

"Not so awful. Just Cossacks. Always a bit greedy for a bit extra. Tax is in skins and furs, you know. The men have a free day a week and must go hunting or trapping. Shermadin escaped while away trapping."

"But the Cossacks *are* awful."

"There are only three of them. We fear them when they are drunk. And the men are frightened for their wives."

"And some prisoners escape completely?"

"Yes, a political last year. Since then all youths between fifteen and twenty-five have to wear leg irons as well."

"I would be insane after one month!" said Boris.

"But sane again if you survived six months," put in the dignified one.

Shermadin's wife was outside asking if she could see Boris and Sergei.

The family came in. The wife, plain, homely, tubby, stooping and with a neckerchief over her head.

She plunged at the feet of Boris and kissed his boots.

"Oh God!" burst Boris. He quickly stooped low to raise her up. But she wanted to kiss his legs. Boris wanted to rush from such a scene.

Then the two children, boy and girl, shy and frightened, kissed his hand. This Boris bore by returning a kiss on their heads. Each then went to Sergei to do the same.

39

Shermadin came forward. "I will tell them all about the mountains," he said. And he was crying.

"And the trees. The great trees," said Boris.

"Oh yes, and the trees, yes, the great trees!"

21

"I'm going to sell Poogavitsa," said Boris. Sergei reared Kukurooza around, the two horses hit, and came to a halt.

"What?"

"How much should I get for him?"

"Nothing."

"Nothing? He's not much to look at, but he must be worth something."

"Nothing."

"Wouldn't you give me something for him?"

"Yes, a kick below your solar plexus. It's nothing, because you are not selling."

"I am."

"If I give you one order only in my life-time it is not to sell Poogavitsa!"

"Look at the way I could not control him after Verkneuralsk. He won't walk. He won't gallop."

"He'll run round the world while you make a cup of tea, as the Mongolian legend says."

"He looks silly. I feel silly. He looks miserable."

"So do you. The pair of you look so bloody miserable, it would seem you have the world's problems on your backs."

"He has the world's problems on his back. But they are my problems. He however was born miserable. Did you ever see such a forlorn face ever?"

"He's got you to carry. You're a couple of misery-bugs. Whatever your problems are, Boris, know that you're in the company of a very lonely creature. Talk to him! You nearly never say a word to each other. You said you couldn't control him and I said keep the reins pulled in lightly. Try talking! He's probably as intelligent as the two of us put together. And he'd give his all for a voice of friendship. But I'm going to tell you something about that nag of yours. So. Uh."

They were blocking the high road but they never budged.

"It won't make any difference. I have decided. I don't feel right. I don't feel even human on it," Boris said.

"Poogavitsa's sire," Sergei began with fervour in his voice, "was part Orlov, part Arabian, and more than one part Bitiug."

"Orlov and Bitiug?"

"Yes. His head is ram-shaped, his chest broad, his croup is sloping, his back is long, his colour sorrel, he could travel eighty miles on one feed. Even a hundred. He could run at full speed without perspiring leaving other horses out of breath and covered in their own foam. He has fine soft ears, steep pasterns, delicate hoofs, every muscle fine and slender and, again, his croup, it is enormously strong. He could carry 150 pounds, always. On such a horse, only twelve and three-quarters hands high, Lieutenant Peschkov rode from inner Siberia to St. Petersburg ten years ago, 6,000 miles, in 193 days. Poogavitsa is cold-blooded. He is one of the very few that are not hot-blooded. If you were dying of thirst, you could cut a vein in his leg, drink the blood, and the wound would heal in no time, and you could quickly be away. People who make war like a secret weapon. Such a horse as Poogavitsa was Genghis Khan's secret weapon. It could continue day and night, its rider asleep on its back. The hordes

41

ravished Russian and Europe and half the human world at twice a day's normal speed. Nothing matched them. Poogavitsa could run without drinking or flagging for 24 hours. Some would argue that at top speed one foot only touches the ground, others would argue that for a fraction of a second no feet are touching the ground. Kukurooza here is fifteen and a half hands high and could not achieve a half your button could."

"Poogavitsa is only eleven and a half hands high," said Boris.

"That's because its mother was a mouse!"

22

Next morning before leaving their bivouac, Boris asked: "Where are you going?"

"To Chita."

"Beyond Baikal?"

"Yes, after Baikal."

"When do you expect to reach there?"

"At the end of next summer."

"Why Chita?"

"No whys."

Then Sergei asked: "Where are you going?"

Boris answered: "To Chita."

"Why?"

"No whys."

"Then perhaps we should shake on it?" asked Sergei.

And they shook hands.

23

That night Boris could get no sleep. The black never left him. The bottomless pit inside him filled with the traumas of Samara.

By day he made all human efforts to put thoughts away, away. By nights, if he slept, his subconscious brought the events crowding back as if sluice-gates had been opened. And this night they took over, woke him up, and if the Borises of the world could cry, Boris's soul cried that night. Black was the night and black was his mind, and black was his soul. . . what was all this 'going to Chita'? Why? Bloody Alexis had let him down. It was all the fault of that insipid priest: he knew, he knew, he knew Boris well enough to know that what was, was not what was meant. No thought of blame for what he himself had done, never; no hint of blame for Zjennia's answers, never; that bloody priest, just that bloody priest.

Boris was discovering that ifs and buts were words from hell's vocabulary. And why, when he tried with all conceivable will-power to forget the events in his awake self, did his subconscious sleeping-self have to pile them back at him? 'Why': that was another word from hell.

Now Zjennia's physical self was creeping in and that fast transformed a dead hell into a live hell. Yes, the physical of it. . .

And the sight of a whole village in manacles. . .

Fancy Boris in manacles making love to Zjennia in manacles. . .

43

Fancy Boris in prison for life – and no sex. . .

What sort of a world is this?

The moon had gone. The stars had gone. In the distance where the black of the heaven joined the grey of the earth, a slit appeared and a new day pushed a white glove through.

And a rabbit appeared. Jumping. Then another. Then such a game as Boris never knew existed. A hundred rabbits in the eerie first light, jumping; fifty jumping with fifty others trying to over jump them, leap-frog style. And each time trying to do it higher.

Rabbit for breakfast? Boris took his gun.

There were a few mounds, a few birches, sedge and reeds, and all else just a play-ground for the rabbit kingdom. A tinkly sound and he heard a stream. Boris went to it. Bubbling away and stones leading into it.

Boris rested his gun and went on the stones to wash. And fish came jollying by. He pounced, caught one, wriggled with it. There was a ridiculous play-about as the fish slid from him, then he just managed to fling it to the shrub. Then a second one. 'So, Sergei my friend, again it's perch for breakfast,' and Boris glanced at the rabbits and winked at them and called to them that there would be no disturbance of their morning frolics, please to continue, he was so glad not to have spoiled their morning.

As he started the fire with dried birch bark, he felt the new-born day mocked him; his heart fled back over the Urals and an arm went with it and reached out for the shoulder of his soft warm beloved.

24

As they rode off the sun came up and filled the opening eye of morning, and the sky lifted up its last lid and yellow streamed through.

Landscape neverchanging, neverending. At rare times, a clump of birch, a clump of larch. Space everlasting, landscapes boundaried only by horizons, then a moorhen explodes and catapults to heaven and announces himself king.

A ripple in a passing stream sings Siberia, a reed rustling says hello to God, a lone bush sighs that history passed it by. Landscape is the Lord and the World, and Boris and Sergei two ants upon it.

The pair rode in silence. Once Sergei said: "How can this steppe be so flat yet end by touching the sky? How can it be that by the time we have reached the horizon, the horizon has disappeared?"

Then a smudge of cattle across a sweep of sand signified that a change was on its way. A tumbrel from one side and two lineikas – low carts built of logs – from the other, both converging on to the dust road, showed a build-up was afoot. Sheep, then more cattle, men in long blouses with belts at their waists, women with kerchiefs about their heads, bent backs and incongruous bundles. . . yes, there was one more river to cross.

And Boris and Sergei became men again and the landscape got telescoped down to being just a back-drop for the crossing of the Isset.

And when they reached the river it was truly to marvel where a multitude had come from. Out of the corners of nowhere a coagulated mass of bent men, bent women, hens, pigs and goats, multifarious packages wrapped in cloth and string, Russians, Mongolians, Buriats; a Khirghis with a turban, and with a horned ram, a wonder of creation, two brodyagi. . .

"Are they brodyagi?" asked Boris.

Sergei nodded yes.

"Who will they prey on?"

"The weakest," said Sergei. "Nothing will happen on the ferry. Afterwards. So. If I was the Khirghis I would worry about that ram. These are no fools here. The weakest will band together. It's to get to some shelter together before nightfall. The Khirghis is wily, he's seen them. He's a fine fellow. And he has two knives. So."

Children were playing. The ferry could be seen in the distance coming over. A boy bobbed up and spoke to Boris. Boris could not understand him. Suddenly Boris felt human. A tick of warmth came to his blood. What was the boy saying? He looked at the boy, at the eyes, brown, laughing, quizzical: "God, I'm a human being!" Boris said half-aloud. A little line of warm blood ran through his system, like a train over a disused railway track – it was ridiculous – he felt human! The boy left, but waved back. Boris had a coin ready. The boy waved again. Boris waved back strongly. He pointed out the coin. But the boy had found friends.

The ferry arrived: a small steamer pulling three log rafts. A deluge got off to let a multitude on. Siberia was overcrowded! From nowhere, there was a mad rush. A crowd carrying bedding, bundles of clothes, jangling kettles, bread wrapped in old linen, sheaves of woodcocks, partridges, pheasants, one wizened old man with a big dried flapping fish, the tail of which slip-slapped the faces of all that passed it by: the whole horde making an insane rush all at the same time to get on a boat which everyone knew had no intention of leaving for hours, the captain

46

– if that's what he could be called – and his crew of two – if that's what they were – being the first to disappear and no one knew when they would emerge again. It was as if Moscow was burning behind them and Napoleon would only let one last group out: yet everyone knew time did not count in Siberia and there was always room, even if sardines might have argued there wasn't.

Sergei said: "Once I was in Mongolia and there was to be a wrestling match. 200,000 came to the valley where it was to be held. And yet there are only one million people in that whole vast country. How are such things possible? Two miles on from the other side of the Isset, you'll find that if you shout your head off there'll be nobody around to hear you."

The ferry was two hours in leaving. Even the goats and the cows were beginning to look upon the rafts as home. No one now was in a hurry. Fires were lit in braziers, schasliks were on their way, tea was simmering, a small knot of peasants called the brodyagis over and gave them food.

"Clever," said Sergei. "That's well done."

Nobody knew where the captain had gone to and no one worried. The boat and the three rafts had become home. There was quarrelling, abuse, laughter, shouting, argument, joy: and around the whole assemblage a noose of camaraderie.

The brodyagis looked like heathen cut-throats, but Sergei said: "Let's go." And Boris and he crossed over rafts and to the two almost sub-human villains and Sergei said: "We have a half chicken if it would help you. Take it with you." And he took out a half chicken from his knapsack.

They took it.

They were Russians.

"There's not much food in these parts," said Sergei. "I'm from Moscow."

"So's Jakob," said one. "I'm from Kazan. We are now from the tin mines at Omsk. I have a wife in Moscow."

They smelt abominably. They looked capable of any crime: but how much of the look was from deprivation?

Sergei said to Boris: "Such things must be done. And the wise peasants started it. We are all in this bloody world together."

One of the two came back and touched Sergei on the shoulder. "We want to be imprisoned for the winter. Where do you suggest?"

"Cheliabinsk," said Sergei. "If you say you are politicals the governor can get a stipend from the Czar for your keep. If you chance your luck and say you are dangerous politicals you'll come off better still."

It was a gruff, rough meeting. But in the whole vast Russian Empire it was always something special to have rubbed shoulders with a man from Moscow.

On the other side of the Isset, the boy waved a good-bye to Boris. And Boris waved back.

25

It happened overnight. Boris and Sergei went to sleep in the summer and woke up in the winter.

In these parts autumn or spring lasted two hours, or two days, or – but nearly never – two weeks. A longish summer was followed by a much longer winter with spring and autumn saying Hallo in between. In many of these parts they say life was two thirds snow and one third mosquitoes.

Thin snow lay everywhere. How silent is a world where snow falls upon snow.

"Hope it hasn't come too early," said Sergei. "For Shermadin."

"Shermadin?"

"I had arranged for him to ride shot-gun on the Post Coach to Ufa. He was a master marksman in Georgia. So. They need a master-shot with them when they run the money through. It's for the Tobolsk government. So."

"Shermadin? Who knows? Does he know?"

"So. No. The Bank of Cheliabinsk will contact the Elders at the convict colony. Everyone knows of Shermadin's virtuosity. So."

"But Shermadin's manacles?"

"They won't hinder. So."

"But people will see them?"

"People are used to seeing them. I hope the snow is not too early for him."

"Shermadin will see the Urals? The mountains?"

"So."

"What are you, Sergei Alexandrovitch? A Jesus Christ or something?"

"I'm a criminal on the run."

"Are you? And no whys?"

"No whys."

"So am I," said Boris. "A criminal on the run. And no whys either."

"Then perhaps we had better shake hands again?"

They did. "So that makes two of us," said Boris.

"Three of us," said Sergei.

"Three of us?"

"Jesus Christ was a criminal on the run, too," said Sergei.

"Really? Then let's watch out we don't get crucified!" And Boris tried a smile, but his face cracked. In all these weeks had not smiled once, and now his face cracked at the event.

26

They were lucky after a blizzard to ride into some hills, and in the hills to discover caves. One of them gave the feeling that it had been occupied before. There were planks of wood in it and some tackle too.

Thus, for one night at least, they would get shelter.

They made a fire and ate. It was cold but they had protection from the wind which, if a man got caught in it, could double the cold.

Boris slept long and on awakening was surprised to see that Sergei was not in the cave. Boris went to the cave's entrance and saw Sergei hopping about in the distance over an iced lake. The wind had abated. The air was crisp, and the sun shone through, though whether or not the sun could be accredited with any heat, that would be difficult to say.

Sergei appeared with four bream and a very odd contraption.

"Once more, fish for breakfast!" And Sergei was proud of himself, though a man would have to know him to know that he was registering pride. But how can a man get fish out of ice?

"How the hell?. . . And from under the ice?" Boris asked.

Sergei shook his head from side to side and came out with no explanations. "A fire. A fire," is all he said.

A fire was made and firstly tea. Many Russians are married to tea and Sergei was one.

Then the cooking of the so fresh fish.

Then Boris wandered off. He found the frozen lake and marked out on it a crude circle large as a large room. Around it were a dozen holes at equi-distance, holes the size of plates.

He returned and found Sergei's contraption-apparatus in the cave. There was a net and twelve pikes, not more than two feet long. "Tell me," he said, "tell me a little of this magic."

Sergei explained, grudgingly: "You stuff the whole lot down one hole, the current floats all except the one stick you hold to the next hole, you heave one up; it floats on. When you have all twelve down the fish swim into the circular net. Then you pull the poles back one by one, and at the original opening you heave the whole lot up, and there's almost always a catch."

A poor explanation. But Boris knew he wouldn't be getting any more for now. Next time he'd watch for himself.

"How did you make the holes in the ice?"

Sergei picked up a small handsaw, gave it a kiss and packed it away.

Boris left to feed the horses which had also been sheltered from the worst of the wind. A cry was heard. Boris rushed round. Sergei had climbed up outside the cave to far above it, then taken a terrible fall. "Get me to the cave," he said. Sergei was in great pain. He quickly took a heavy swill of vodka. "I think it's my hip," he said. "It's serious."

For half an hour the two were silent. There was pain, and there were the efforts of stifle groans.

"You better teach me that fishing trick and we'll get a lot of bream in stock," said Boris.

"Boris, friend," said Sergei. "It's more serious than that. You should go on."

"Never in a thousand years!"

"Give me five minutes," said Sergei. "To think."

51

Five minutes were gone. It continued into ten. Then Sergei said:

"Boris, this is not a novelette, this is not the theatre, this is not where heroics and heroic friendship shows noble. This is life. And life is a practicable thing. And sense will get us further than sentiment. Split our food stock in two. You can leave me the vodka. Do not get more fish: it takes time and you would need my guidance for your first catch and I cannot move that far. Bring Kukurooza to the cave. He will squeeze in. If I have to, I will kill him for food. The road is marked all the way. Where there are trees you will find, at twenty pace distances, ribbons at hip height, if no ribbons then paint. If no trees, then cairns, but they can be fifty paces apart. Never go outside the lines, you cannot know what is beyond the edge covered by snow. If a mist comes or visibility is obscure I implore you to stop: never move off course or take chances. Wait: even if it is for two days, wait for light. There is a proverb, 'all roads lead to the capital': well, I cannot promise you St. Petersburg, but no road leads to nowhere. Somewhere you must meet up with someone. Save yourself. If you have strength, come back and you will find me. These are the first caves in the first hills for hundreds of miles, therefore the last for you when coming back. But I will need a sledge, or a lineiaka. I cannot mount a horse: and if I could and were to fall off, it would finish me. I have broken or fractured the femur, the thigh-bone, just below the hip."

"Now give me five minutes," said Boris. "To think."

And he too, took ten.

"I'm going," he said and went for Kukurooza.

When he returned Sergei said: "No sentiment, Boris. Just leave. No words. We are practical people."

Boris gave him a look and nodded. He put all things around Sergei in logical order and, nearest to him, his gun. He put more oats near Kukurooza.

The two men nodded.

Boris mounted Poogavitsa and left.

27

The air cried crisp and the way rode fair. The hills faded behind and the steppes opened their flat mouth to let in the giant on his midget horse.

All day they rode. The snow sucked all sound in and silence was God.

One stop, and that a brief one. Boris carried raw meat with him. He took some quick mouthfuls, then said 'Why not?' and to test the theory he put some beef between the saddle and Poogavitsa's flanks and would see if his own weight-heat would cook it.

All day, and not a soul. Not a cart, not a farm, not one log cabin. A flock of swallows, over-greedy from their feed of mosquito in the north, double speeding it south east. Tell-tale footmarks in the snow, hares, foxes, field mice? And once, an elk? But all had left their visiting cards only and he saw or heard no animal.

As he was thinking that night would soon be with him, the gods seemed with him too for he rode into some copses of pine and birch. This posed a problem. Here was a slight shelter and some timber for a fire, but if he continued till nightfall where would he be then? If the temperature was minus five now, it would be nothing less than minus ten in the night. He felt he had a call from Sergei for common-sense and though all driving forces in him screamed for charging on, he halted.

It was little protection, the trees were sparse, but there was timber: "Poogavitsa, we're staying."

He tore at the birch bark – nothing started a fire like

birch bark – he fiercely broke off twigs and even a branch, chose his spot and tea was on its way.

He fed Poogavitsa – how clever Sergei was at choosing oats. He had left most of the purchasing to Sergei, but Boris had noticed how well he chose. And a shrewd bargainer too. Most purchases were in barter and tobacco and spirits were the certain sells. Sergei was always buying tobacco though he smoked little.

Night was falling and a wind was rising. Damn it, a wind! It howled round the trees like a wild animal searching. Soupy darkness travelled with it. Could it be a storm? No, just night in a hurry to settle.

No stars, no moon, just patches of doom-like, tomb-like gloom filling up the empty spaces where day had been.

'I'll need more warmth.' Boris was talking to himself. He began stuffing his schuba with pine needles. Except for the extremities, the fingers, the nose, the ears, only the chest was important. Indeed it was everything. He doubled his measurements with his intake of needles. 'I had better be careful,' he said 'else Poogavitsa will not recognise me.'

He was about to sleep when his fire melted the snow crystals on the high birch beside him, poured down a shower, and the fire was out! Blue smoke, and water.

He was up like a shot and tearing round as the fire-light died, fetching new bark and twigs. He attempted another fire away from the first, but bungled it. His curses woke heaven up.

'My priorities,' he said.'Save Sergei, save my life, save warmth.'

The temperature was dropping. Under twenty and he had to beware. It was under ten already. The wind. . . yes, the fattest tree would shield him slightly. The trees were slender and not easy to distinguish, but he assured himself of one, brought his things against it, and settled there.

Everything was possible if prepared. Even a snow protection could be built. A good fire. . . but he had made no skilled protection. 'Sergei is going to live! So that means I must too.' Sleeping at such temperatures and a man can freeze to death and merely not wake up.

Boris knew his danger point. It was that figure, that twenty degrees below zero. And it would be approaching that before this night was over. He must keep awake. Then he would have to ride through the morrow tired. But he dare not chance sleep. Sergei, you will live! And Poogavitsa and I will save you. Oh for the hide of Poogavitsa! He's probably in dreamland now. How tough that hide. He had seen horses withstand seventy below. Forty was common in Samara.

Even if freezing starts with pain, it continues sweetly. A tiredness overtakes a person and he slides into a sleep from which he never wakes up.

Boris rose from his tree and walked around. He felt he should tighten his schuba and took off a mitten and, in a flash thrust it back on again. Two minutes of that and his fingers would be gone. He ran around. He bashed his finger tips against a tree trunk, then squashed them under his boots. Must keep the circulation going.

Fourteen hours of this? And only one gone yet? Or was it two?·'Priorities – keep alive till morning. Then save Sergei's life. Sorry Sergei, the priorities have been reversed.'

No moon. No star. A murky indigo above and the dark trees just darker than the night.

The wind whistled at odd times as if a spirit of a lost ice-age was passing through, but it did not grow too fierce, and in snatches when Boris sat against his tree trunk he felt in a wind-proof ice-box, and it was a relief from the added torment of the blast.

Every quarter of an hour he forced himself up from his coma-cocoon and walked or ran around, protecting his nose, his ears, and especially his hands.

'Might as well go on,' he said. 'We'll feel the way.' But he had made a vow to Sergei to resist just that, and he held on to himself.

Three hours gone now? Even four? 'The whole of Siberia sleeping except poor bloody Boris champing the snows up in a tiny wood no map could have put a name to. Feeling as cold as fear. Bloody fire. Bloody Alexis, it's all your fault!' And the priest would have caught his wrath and felt it through the distances, except that Boris checked his spleen and gave all his mind to staying alive.

Five hours? Six? 'Look, there's a star! Hi, star, are you cold or hot up there? Must be either too cold, or too hot. If only I could be too hot! How can Siberia sleep in this cold? Does Siberia freeze to death every night? The stillness sucks you in, sucks you down, like a bath ingurgitating without a plug. Only this bath is blocked up with ice. Another star! I'm not alone. Two stars up there, me down here. Three of us, as Sergei said. What has wicked 'criminal' Sergei done to bring down the wrath of the Czar of all the Russias? And what nefarious activity is he up to in Chita?'

Boris returned to his tree and sat against it. 'I heard of a man who escaped and was being hunted in Siberia and a shrub hid him from his captors. And he fell in love with that shrub. Forever and ever. He was still talking about it fifty years later. Did the shrub know? If this tree wasn't so heavy, I'd take it along with me. Nice thing, a tree. They say a man shelters under a tree when in trouble, and cuts it down when he isn't. I think nine hours have gone and I should close my eyes.'

He did so resting on his haunches, so that if he fell he'd wake up.

"Hallo," he said out loud. No echo. The snow swallowed the sound. "I'm alone in a lonely place. I should be in a warm bed!" And he bloody nearly cried.

'Unfriendly, black, satanic night. Where this idea that Hell is hot? Hell is god-damn cold. Cold is a terribly foul animal that gets through and eats Boris alive. And from inside me, I have to keep it from coming in, and if I doze off it will sinister in. Ten hours now? I am not beaten yet, but nearly am. I'll go to Poogavitsa.'

He found him. Still as death, standing there like a marble monument to a tiny horse. 'Mustn't disturb him.' And he went away. And he beat his hands, and his arms, and tried to run but he found he was too weary.

'A funny thing! I'm in a wilderness of emptiness, yet at the end of that copse that way and,' turning round, 'the other way, and turning again on either side of the road, there's a wall. I'm surrounded on all four sides by a wall. That's because I know I will not go outside that space. Not outside this copse, not off this road. That is a very interesting wall. It is a wall. Yet it isn't a wall. Yes, that's a very funny thing. In a way, I've got a home. Brodyagis must often have that feeling.'

He was tired. Was it lack of sleep, or was it cold? He rested against the tree standing up, with his gun under his chin as he had seen soldiers do. He closed his eyes and if his head fell he must hurt his chin and wake up.

But after an aeon of time which might have been a minute or might have been an hour, he fell to the ground. 'Missed my chin,' he said, and forced himself up. 'I'm not bloody well doing that again.'

He counted to a hundred. Then down to nought, backwards. Then he tried counting again, but he was too tired.

He noticed the cold was fiercer still. That held hope. The coldest hour is before the dawn. "Poogavitsa, get ready. We're off at light. We'll eat later. A bit of warmth first."

Yes, yes, yes, the petrified white carpet beneath him was getting whiter. "Get ready, Poogavitsa!"

He tried to whistle. Too much effort. An empty stomach didn't sanction such a prank. He fought the sleepiness like a tiger. It got at him but he would not surrender. His head was blocked with fatigue. No, he would not surrender. One last sitting against the tree? No, he would not surrender. He went round and round in a tiny circle and glanced at every turn at the east.

He would not surrender! 'Sergei, this night is for you. What have they done with the dawn? God, wake up, and send the bloody dawn!'

He went round in ever faster circles but at a terrible stoop.

It was here! Yes? No? Yes! "Poogavitsa, we're off in five minutes. I've made it! Thank you, tree!" He put both his mitts on the tree as a blessing. "Look after yourself without me."

Poogavitsa gave a half shake of his head and was ready.

They had left.

28

The morning was not difficult. The day's freshness kept sleep at bay.

Siberia had five million square miles and five million people: that is, one per square mile. Where were they? Siberia had four million horses? Where are your friends, Poogavitsa? And two million houses or cabins. Have they all been pulled down?

The wind did not know whether to blow or not. But when it did, it blew into him. Which, as Boris knew, was prevalent, so at least he could not feel cheated. There were places in Siberia where it blew the whole year through. He had met one traveller who had said he had not been out of a wind for three years and it was sending him crazy.

As the day wore on, deterioration set in. The sky took on a dun grey, then a doom grey, an icy draught came with it, tiredness crept all over Boris, and he knew he was in for another trial.

If any wave of the landscape, or another group of trees, or a forest (!) or a house (!) came he would sink into it, build every security possible, then pray, then sleep. Tiredness crept into him like possessiveness. He slept a little, riding upright. He remembered the meat he had put under the saddle. He went to raise himself to feel underneath him: something seemed locked, he could not raise the saddle, he even had difficulty transferring his hand, he was half-comatose, half-dreaming, he felt there should be a nightmare lurking somewhere and he should be aware of it, he should rally, he tried, something he should be aware of, was he freezing? falling asleep? He must get off and exercise. But he continued. But he must dismount. Something had gone wrong. Sergei, yes, he could not fail Sergei.

'Let's get off and sort this out.' He thought he pulled the reins, he was not sure. Poogavitsa still seemed running. Was it dark? No. But getting dark. Must stay on the road. Yes, must stop.

He went slugged with cold.

He passed out. Bolt upright.

Poogavitsa ran.

Icicles were forming. The temperature kept falling all the time. Boris could not fall. He was frozen to his horse. Icicles were drooping. He had to do something. He knew he had to do something. But one minute more and he was absolutely asleep.

Icicles. Like a candelabra he was becoming.

And night was there. And the little horse ran on.

One grotesque frozen chess-piece, a knight on a horse, all night, through the stillness, then a blizzard, then a whistling wind down this Siberian highway, then a howl as of ice-castle werewolfs let out to roam, then a blizzard again blowing scurry, scurry, razor-knife paring their faces, Poogavitsa, head still forward, running, Boris, aware of events just for moments when he regained consciousness, then, finding himself in a whirl he could not understand, returning to Morpheus. 'Sergei, Sergei, we are trying. . . trying. . .'

All night, through the too-lost world, on a road that even Siberia seemed to have discarded.

All night, frozen as one grotesque chessman across a deserted chessboard.

All night.

29

As a shaft of daylight broke, Poogavitsa left the high road, ran a quarter of a mile into a field now overcoated in snow, went up to a yurt,* unbelievably opened the hanging hides that served as entrance, entered and stopped dead.

The alarmed inhabitants raised themselves from sleep on to their arms and stared amazed.

Transfixed, most stared on. One squat middle-aged man rose and went towards the apparition.

"Hot water," he said.

And two women stirred and put on the pot.

*Yurt: Large and solid tent

The squat figure took a stool and mounted it, and with some rag, moistened the icicles hanging about the apparition's eyes. Gently and very carefully he cleared all space around the eyes, then, with fresh water and fresh rag he began about the lips.

The eyes seemed to open. There was a stir among all present, an excited yet subdued hum and wonder.

Soon the whole face was cleared and the eyes were still open and the eye-lids blinked.

Then the Buriat, for he was a Buriat, added snow to the boiling water, felt it, poured more snow in, then, satisfied, picked up the whole bucket and threw it at the chessman. Soon both horse and rider were be-stirring themselves and the yurt became electrically excited.

Two more buckets-full and the work was ended. Boris shook himself, mesmerised, but found his shackles mostly gone. People, mostly small people, were round him knocking off the last dissolving icicles.

Word had reached other yurts and newcomers came pouring in.

Boris dismounted and people were clapping their hands, tittering, laughing outright, chattering, excited as monkeys.

The leader spoke. Boris could not understand.

"Russian," he said.

"Russian?" That they understood, and someone rushed off for someone who spoke Russian.

Boris stood bemused. "It's morning?" he asked. But no one understood him. "It's morning? It's morning?" one or two childishly repeated. The whole tent was agog. Many were inspecting the horse. One had fetched food for it.

"Can I?" asked Boris, and took the sack and put it over Poogavitsa's head.

30

A day later all preparations had been made to retrace the road to Sergei.

The leader wished to leave Poogavitsa behind.

"No," said Boris and cloth pads were put on his horse's hoofs.

There was a sledge with a dog team and four riding horses.

After two days Boris felt the hills approaching among which would be the cave where Sergei should be.

He conferred with the leader and the interpreter, and all agreed there was no other range before the long steppe westwards. The Buriats were short, square-headed, square-bodied and never stopped smiling. If there was childish stupidity among them, not so with their leader, who, in fact, never smiled.

Boris was certain they had found the range. Snow fell lightly like giant leopard paws falling on earth.

There were no caves. Boris turned left off the road, which he remembered was the direction they had been down before.

He shouted out. All shouted out. It was as if they were calling for a team of Sergeis. Silence reigned. And the snow fell on. Confetti – without the bridegroom.

There were no caves of any sort.

"We must continue on," said Boris, but felt a gnaw of panic inside him. He went with Poogavitsa up and down, up and down, beside the hills. There was no path. Then he dismounted. He walked back to the sledge. Tension built up inside him.

There was nothing. They must continue westwards, and hope. . . but, it was uncanny. . . Boris could swear it was right.

Poogavitsa had moved inward, inward towards the hill.

The leader and Boris went to the horse, but had decided to leave for the next range, however far it was.
. Poogavitsa was difficult to budge. The horse put its head to the ground, then up again. Funny old horse.

"Let's go," said the two men, but Poogavitsa was hard to move.

"What's that?" asked the leader, pointing with a stick.

"Just a ribbon," said Boris. "They mark these roads with ribbons."

"The ribbons on this road are red. That is blue."

The two went closer.

"It's tied to the end of a bloody gun barrel!" cried Boris.

They tore at the snow, and the others came running. More and more of the barrel was uncovered.

"The snow is loose," said the leader. "Be careful and stand-back." A crude shovel was called for and the snow removed at arm's length.

"The butt of the gun!" cried Boris, and he was beside himself.

"Careful! Careful!" came the warning. "The snow is too loose."

Ten minutes and a mircle of miracles. Sergei was there. Mostly prone and saying: "So there you are Boris."

The Buriats danced near to hysteria. Clapped, tittered, shouted, brought food, cheered, jogged, six happy maniacs around two friends who in their hearts were even more joyous still.

It was difficult to get the story out of Sergei. Over the days the facts emerged: Sergei with great effort had got

63

the timber over to him that had been left behind in the cave by an earlier occupant. With his hand-saw he had carved himself a sort of splint. He had torn a shirt in shreds and used it as strings and fixed the splint. He then took vodka and slept. Waking he found his leg easier. A woodcock came outside the cave and settled. Sergei shot it. Another came. He shot that. After six hours or so, Sergei thought he'd chance his leg and collect his spoils, using the rifle as a crutch. He reached the birds, fastened them around his waist, but a surprisingly heavy slide of snow, a minor avalanche, caught him and buried him – sideways.

Under the snow, he quickly cleared the space around his mouth, spat with his hand underneath, so that, from the fall of his spittle he could discover which was 'up', he then thrust his gun through and realised the end reached good air, lowered it, tied on a tear of his blue shirt, and thrust the gun up again.

He found, yes, he was buried 'at the slant'. He could not reach his legs, he cleared a passage for his hands to his waist, realised that any multiple action of his with the snow might plunge him into new, most certainly, worse trouble. Then he panicked for two hours and felt as crazed as he had ever felt.

"And for food?"

"I cut slices off my woodcocks. The snow kept them fresh. I knew they'd last me a long time. Water was a little snow itself."

After the hours of panic had gone, he settled into his cocoon, the snow all round kept him warm, and he had complete faith that Boris would find him. His optimism was, to Boris, insane, but to Sergei it had been 'practical'.

"And Kukurooza?"

"Ah, yes, Kukurooza. We have to find the cave."

And the busy-bee Buriats, all joy, went fiercely about

64

unearthing the cave. One found it by thrusting a pick-axe into snow which made no resistance, cried out, and to this day reminds all his children and his children's children, that the horse and the cave were of his finding.

31

Vassili, the interpreter, was a pinch of a man. He had a face like a rat, he was always looking down as if ashamed, yet he was bright, sharp, alert. He did not look one per cent Buriat, let alone fifty per cent. His Russian was difficult to follow, yet perhaps it was his manner, rather than his speech. He was a busy-body but, for some reason, he was furtive and impossible to fathom.

There was a reason why the small party wanted to rush their journey home, but Boris and Sergei could not find the reason out. Vassili made fussy answers, but no complete answers.

"Is this not paining you?" Boris asked Sergei. "Shall I slow them down?"

"The speed suits me," said Sergei. "The sooner I reach warmth, the sooner I can begin to think."

So the party scurried back. The snows swirled, blizzards came and dashed through and between them like wild beasts, the skies looked often ominous and often serene; Sergei's pain was tremendous and arrack became his saviour. The Buriats had spasms of consideration, but their consideration was more for time than for Sergei's leg. Vassili made quick rapid movements of help, but his allegiance was obviously first for his companions and their hurry.

All through the night they travelled, never letting up.

At last their commune was reached and the great yurt gained.

A cheer was their welcome, but very soon the two Russians were left alone with the women and a token of newcomers. Their companions of the road, the leader, and Vassili too, all disappeared.

"They have to prepare," was all that could be learned. And for what they had to prepare still remained a mystery.

Food was made, hot goat, hot fox, black tea with lard and butter in it, kvass* and more arrack; rugs of bear and elk were granted Sergei on a raised palliasse: but the numbers in the yurt got fewer and fewer and the two friends became suspicious and decided to sleep with their pistols at their sides.

Soon night was upon them. People began trickling in and they went straight to their sleeping places. Vassili came and was evasive. He answered their questions with answers which led nowhere and he, also, busied himself with sleep.

Boris would not close his eyes. There was something he could not understand. And his hand would not leave his holster.

32

Boris, this being his second night without sleep, felt re-assured enough when dawn had come without foul play, and he laid aside his revolver and joined with slumber.

*Kvass: a malt drink

But at nine he stirred. He felt the yurt was empty. He sat up on his arms. There was one wizened hag dozing over a pot. Then Vassili came in.

"Vassili," he called. "Come, tell me, where is everyone?"

"At the Tailgan."

"What's that?"

Vassili did not want to answer but quietly said: "The Great Horse Sacrifice."

"Then take me to it!" And Boris had risen.

"No. No."

"Why so?"

"Only Buriats dare be there."

"Is that why you are not there?"

Vassili nodded. "I am allowed to see it. But not to be there."

"Then let me see it! Come! We're going!"

Sergei slept on soundly. Vassili looked disturbed, but was afraid of Boris, and wondered how little of the Sacrifice he need show to appease him.

Boris found Poogavitsa. Vassili had a horse already with feet padded against the snow and ice, and the two rode off.

The Tailgan, the Great Horse Sacrifice, had been the reason for their hurrying home. To have been late for it would have angered the gods: the births of the reindeer, cows, horses, the success of the crops, the births of their sons, all depended on the success of the Tailgan.

Over a large sprawled out area stood thirty yurts and as many log cabins. Before all were burkans. These were headhigh square posts cut at the top at a forty-five degree slope. Hanging near to the necks of the posts were strips of iron, wings of birds, tongues of animals, teeth of wolves and bears, and strips of skin of fox and ermine. These were all offerings to the gods.

Away on a Hill called Uher were fifteen altars and it was there that the sacrifice was held.

Almost the whole settlement had toured in a long dawdling chanting circle past every shrine and burgan pole in the neighbourhood. Sweet tarasun,* sour tarasun and mare's milk was sprayed about the burkans, as the crawl-sprawl of people wound their way up to the altars. The god, the Iron Hero, the Stallion of the Sky, who fed on burning coals and drank lightning, was offered these nourishments symbolically with fires and white spirit, while drums beat to a crescendo and the populace chanted.

Seven horses had already been slaughtered. Only two remained. Nine was the number for the gods. The two remaining were large white mares.

Vassili said that on the Hill stood the Most Splendoured Buildings in Creation, that they were invisible to man. Tarasun, mare's milk, tea, twigs, branches, bushes, iron vessels were being tossed in the air or sprinkled round the fifteen altars, while the drums kept up a fearsome beat. Vassili and Boris had halted by a clump of birch and approached no nearer.

One of the white mares was led between the fires to be purified – nine fires – then sprinkled with milk on its face and hair. Then all present bowed to the ninety-seven Western burkans, then to the four Eastern burkans, then they offered homage to 'the lofty clear heaven', to 'the revered pure earth' then to 'the bull prince father' then to 'the blessed mother who created the Great One' then to 'the hedgehog' then to 'the grandfather bald head' then to 'the creator of cattle' then to 'the golden sorrel' then to the 'deity crooked back'. All these deities were appealed to, that they should listen to their prayers and accept their offerings.

*Tarasun: Alcohol made from fermented mare's milk

The drums stopped.

Four ropes were tied around the fetlocks of the horse, each rope held by four men. Then the front eight men pulled the front legs forward and spreadeagled them apart. Then the back eight men spread out the rear legs backwards and apart. At this the horse fell to its side and was flicked on to its back. A man came with a sharp knife and with one blow made an incision behind the breast bone. He thrust his hand into the opening and seized the heart and wrenched it from its connections. The horse attempted a struggle but was held too tightly and died quickly.

But the second horse at this point regained position enough to bite the ground in agony. A writhing horror twisted across its face like a snake sliding over it. Its teeth bared to a ghastly grin, its eyes became green, then blue. Its expression was of piercing, helpless agony. It groaned in unspeakable anguish.

Distant, squat square-shaped Buriats hurried forward to the white mares, quartered them, separated the flesh from the bones and placed them on the fifteen altars. Fires were freshly lit. Roaring, raving fires: the Iron Hero was hungry.

Flesh was put into iron kettles. And the populace grew animated and thrust forth their prayers. "We have chosen the best tarasun for you, the best meat for you. May we receive your blessing. Create cattle in our enclosures, make our village one mile longer, under our blankets create a son, send rain from heaven, cause much grass to grow. Let no wolves out. Above me be as a coverlet, below me be as a felt bed."

The sky darkened with vultures. Boris remembered that previous short crossing of a river, where out of a seeming nowhere suddenly had come a mass of people. Now, blank skies became blackened with vultures – from where?

The gods were satisfied.

The vultures were satisfied.

The men were satisfied.

"They manage to keep the best tarasun back for themselves," said Vassaili. Could Boris believe his ears? Had Vassili sarcasm inside him?

33

Boris went to Sergei with suggestions for the winter and began by saying: "They invite us to stay. Not just for the winter. Forever!"

"Yes. I know," said Sergei. "Vassili and I are going to Omsk."

Boris suddenly shut up, silent. Vassili and Sergei had planned to go to Omsk? He felt a heavy arrow in him. Since his savage Samara nightmare he had, with the rescuing of Sergei, got a first touch of his old pride returning: he felt the leader, he felt that ideas, organising, and action were his province and that he would be telling Sergei, and Vassili too, what all of them would be doing. 'Zjennia, they've knocked me down again,' he thought. 'Zjennia,' he thought on, 'nothing knocks Boris down.'

But he went away from Sergei and pretended he was preparing tea. And he prepared it in the Russian way, without the lards and the fats and the constant beating in the monstrous churn. He left the tea and went back to Sergei.

"You are going without me?"

"Oh I hope not. You will surely come? You don't want to stay here, do you? There's good winter work in Omsk."

70

Boris returned to his boiling tea.

Again he went back. "How far is Omsk?"

"Three good days."

Boris returned once more to the fire. "First, the facts. I'll square it up with my pride later."

He returned with an iron mug of tea for Sergei, but said he was taking his outside, and he'd be back soon. Boris felt like a boxer who had earlier been unfairly and grotesquely floored, and then while picking himself up had been floored again before he was on his feet. For these months, Boris had not been himself. Boris was all pride, but of a pride of worth, never mean. When he got his pride back, the world would be his again. He had no idea how he would handle the Samara sage. Zjennia: would she be a barb he could never remove from his side? But first, his pride. The first glow of his pride's warmth had touched him in this last week with the rescuing of Sergei. Actually, he knew that, take pride away from himself, and Boris was not Boris any more. He had made his first vow, and that on that night alone with Poogavitsa in that desperate Siberian steppe, he had vowed he would never, ever, allow himself to be manacled again. He only vaguely believed in God, and he had had to have someone or something to vow to. And his belief in God was insufficient for a vow. For a moment he thought of Poogavitsa. The little horse was also not enough. And then, mystery of mysteries, he could not understand why, he had vowed to Zjennia. "Zjennia, I will never be manacled again. I swear it!"

Now he returned to Sergei. "I will come."

"Of course."

It had not been 'of course'! But the first thing Boris knew about pride was that the existence of it must never stop a man doing the right thing. It gnawed him that Vassili and Sergei could talk plans without his being there, but to go to Omsk was an exciting prospect not

71

only for Sergei because of hospitals and doctors, but for Boris too. Boris expected Omsk to be another city as Samara — alas, it wasn't.

34

Vassili was to tell a story. It was the last night before six sledges would leave with Sergei and Boris for Omsk.

Many had come from other yurts and there was an expectancy in the air, for, seemingly, frequently there were these gatherings to hear this half-son tell stories from far and wide, from Yermak to Khabarov, from Mongolia (Buriat land) to the Arctic Ice Forests, from sleepy old bears to magical mice, from heroes to villains with ninety heads.

As seemed to be his nature, Vassili began by staring at the carpets, yet the vitality was there, and the yurt became spellbound. 'I bet' thought Boris 'that Vassili is such that if he was a little rat and met a great lion in a wood, he'd bite the lion on his bum then scamper for his life.'

"There was a young man named Sharau. One day he told his mother that if he had a small sum of money he would make it to a vast sum in the big world. His mother gave him a hundred roubles and he set forth.

"He met a man with a cat under his arm. 'I am taking the cat away to kill it. It fights my dog and always wins,' said the man.

"'Don't kill the cat,' said Sharau, 'I will give you 100 roubles for him.'

"That was an enormous amount of money. 'What joy!' said the man and gave Sharau the cat.

"So Sharau turned to go home as he had no more money. The cat jumped out of his arms and ran off into the woods.

"Sharau returned home and told his mother that he had bought a large storehouse for grain and that if he had another hundred roubles he could do as well again.

"The mother gave him another 100 roubles and he set forth.

"He met a man carrying a dog. 'I am going to kill this dog. He fights my cat, steals its food, and I have no peace.'

"'Don't kill your dog,' said Sharau. 'I will give you 100 roubles for him.' But would it be enough? For he had only just recently given as much for a cat?

"The man could not believe his luck. He gladly gave over his dog.

"The dog struggled to get away from Sharau's clutch, jumped down, and ran off into the woods.

"When Sharau returned his mother asked him 'What have you done with the money?'

"'I bought rich grain and filled our storehouse and now I wish to marry. The Magpie Khan – Sazrai Khan – lives two steps from heaven and has a daughter Sarung-Gohung – a bird only known in paradise – and I wish to marry her.'

"The mother travelled to two steps from heaven and met the Sazrai Khan. 'You have a beautiful daughter,' said the mother, 'and I have a clever son with the largest grain-store on our earth. Let us become related each to each.'

"'If your son will build a silver bridge from your yurt to my yurt he will have my daughter. If he does not I will have his head.'

"The mother went home crying. 'You must find another bride, Sharau. The Magpie-Khan says you are only a merchant and must build a silver bridge from our yurt to his yurt to win his daughter. And if you do not he will have your head.'

"'Then I had better run away and keep my head,' said Sharau and left his mother.

"Far away after nine hills he came to the woods where he had lost his dog and he met the dog and said 'Oh dog! what can I do? I must build a silver bridge from my yurt to the yurt two steps from heaven to win the beautiful Sarung-Gohung. And I have no money. What shall I do?'

"'Take this ring,' said the dog. 'Return to your yurt. Look at the sun. Making nine circles with your hand, say, while turning round, 'Let a bridge of silver be built this night from my yurt to that of Sazrai Khan.'

"This Sharau did. And when he awoke next morning there stood the silver bridge. He went to it, took an axe, and pretended to work on it. Sazrai Khan came to look at the bridge and only said: 'Why are you so long at the work? Were not the long night hours sufficient?'

"'I have built it complete in one night,' said Sharau, resting down his axe. 'If there is any man can build it faster, he can have your daughter.'

"'We will have the wedding in seven days,' said the Khan, and left.

"After the wedding Sarung-Gohung went to live with her husband and was soon full of complaints. 'You can build a bridge of silver in one night yet you live in this wretched yurt,' she said.

"Sharau said nothing about his ring and was very careful to keep it hidden. At night he slept with it in his mouth. One night he coughed and it fell out and he grasped it quickly. Sarung-Gohung teased him unmercifully, wanting to know why he slept with a ring in his mouth. At last he told her about the silver bridge and that the ring had magic if held to the sun and nine circles were made. She teased him even more unmercifully until he gave her the ring to guard as she said he might lose it.

74

"Sarung-Gohung had a secret lover over the sea and next morning as the sun rose she tested the power of the ring and at the magical moment of the ninth circle she was in the arms of her lover.

"When Sharau woke and found his wife had gone he went to the Khan and said: 'See what a wife your daughter has proved to be.'

"'I gave you my daughter,' said the Khan. 'If you haven't her now that means you have killed her.'

"And he threw Sharau into a dungeon. The Khan said: 'I will wait seven days. If my daughter does not return by then that means you most certainly have cut off her head. Then I will cut off yours.'

"Sharau had nothing to eat and he was bound hand and foot. On the second night he heard a scratching and soon the cat came towards him. 'You are a fool,' said the cat. 'You should not have told about the ring. Your wife is away in another kingdom and has married her lover. I will go off and counsel with the dog.'

"The dog said to the cat 'Jump on my back and we will go to the kingdom over the sea.'

"In that kingdom the cat caught a mouse who lived in the yurt with the lovers.

"The cat said 'If you do not do as we wish we will cut off your head. In the mouth of Sarung-Gohung where you live is a gold ring. You must get that gold ring. That way you can keep your head.'

"The mouse worked hard all night and at last burrowed a hole through to the room where Sarung-Gohung slept with her lover. Just at daybreak the mouse crept up to the bed, jumped on it, crept up to its mistress's face, tickled it underneath the chin, Sarung-Gohung sneezed, the ring fell to the floor, the mouse snatched at it and was out through its hole like a flea being chased by a tornado.

"The cat went back to the dog, jumped on its back and

75

they set off for their own kingdom as quick as rain does fall upon earth.

"But then the cat and the dog quarrelled. The dog wanted to carry the ring. The cat said: 'Whoever heard of a dog running with its mouth anything but open? My mouth is small, and I keep it shut. So I will carry the ring.'

"But when they came to cross the sea the cat sneezed and the ring fell out and dropped in the water and it sank to the bottom.

"'Now Sharau will die,' they both agreed.

"They came on land and felt hungry and caught a fish and as they were eating it the ring fell out of the fish.

"The cat jumped on the back of the dog and away they sped through nine forests, over nine mountains, across the land of nine round lakes. The dog said 'Hold as tight as you can. We still might just be in time.' He ran as no dog has ever run before. He ran through the night and when daylight came he asked for the ring and wished nine times but it was already the morning of the eighth day, and they had arrived at that very same last hour in the dungeon of Sazrai Khan.

"But there below, there was no sun in the dungeon. 'That's no matter,' said the cat to distressed Sharau. 'Face the West and turn nine circles with nine wishes, and you will be where you wish to be.'

"And Sharau wished to be in the Khan's presence. And he said to the Khan 'My wife is living with a lover in a kingdom across the sea. I want you to get her back.'

"'You have killed your wife,' said the Khan, 'if not, bring her here yourself and I will spare your head.'

"The young man made nine circles to the sun with the ring and immediately Sarung Gohung and her lover were present.

"'Now,' said Sharau to the Khan. 'What will you do?'

"'I will do to them what I was about to do to you,' and he cut off both their heads."

35

Boris led the six sledges on Poogavitsa. In the first sledge was Sergei in a complicated system of comfort with furs and rugs. The journey was hard and Sergei had to resort to arrack to get respite from his pains.

In the last sledge was Vassili.

Most Buriats were going to Omsk for trading and most of the trading was with grain and hides.

A village was reached: a white-washed gilt-spired cupolaed-church hemmed about by rubbish is a village. Then it was as quickly behind them.

A cry went up from the last sledge. They were being attacked. The cry took some time before it reached up to Boris who scurried back.

He was too late.

Two brodyagi had rushed upon the last sledge. While one caused havoc the other grabbed a sack and the two fled.

No one was hurt. No hides were taken. And no grain. One small sack was missing and the brodyagi had disappeared in the birch wood on snow shoes.

Vassili was even less communicative about that little sack than he had been about anything else. Boris did not know it, but that little sack was the reason behind Vassili's planning this whole journey to Omsk, using Sergei's broken thigh as a cover.

Vassili showed that he had grabbed one of the two thieves and torn off a piece of his coat.

Next day Boris came upon a body lying a little away from the edge of their road.

The sledge-train stopped. Vassili produced the piece of old coat he had grabbed and, yes, that was their attacker, and he was dead. A search was made about the place but nothing but that one body was found.

"And that?" asked Boris. He pointed to many hoof marks further on.

"A posse with horses," said Vassili. "Could have been six. What happened to this one's companion?"

There was no sign of anything or anyone else.

The next day. More dead bodies and two dead horses. No packages. But again, without any explanation, Vassili took souvenirs of cloth, of stirrup, of buckle, even buttons, from the murdered forms.

Boris wanted to know more. But Vassili again gave evasive answers. He was the King of Evasive Answers.

Just before Omsk Sergei called for Boris. "Ask for the offices of the Akmolinsk Territory Gazette. Then ask for the Editor Timor Timorovitch Radek to come down and see us."

"There are newspapers in Omsk?"

"There are four. And they all know me." And Sergei winked. Was it a wink? Yes, because a flicker of a smile followed it. 'Sergei, you are a mystery man,' thought Boris. 'Vassili, you are a mystery man.' But then, 'perhaps I am too? We are just a collection of men, each locked in his own secret, helping out in an experiment of life on a minor planet in a remote galaxy.'

"I am glad I met up with you," said Sergei.

And Boris was happy to hear that coming out of the blue.

"Boris," continued Sergei. "You don't want to spend the winter in prison, do you?"

"No. Why?"

"I could get you locked up in some sort of comfort. And with nothing to do. But I'm sure you would rather be active. We'll speak with Timor Timorovitch. Is hunting in your line?"

78

"Yes."
"We'll speak with Timor."

36

At the end of a birch wood a clearing was reached. Fields of snow like giant ermine carpets strained across the table flat horizon. A sky of slate, which was God's ceiling, elongated itself above the carpets, and Omsk, pencil-thin, like a toy town, tried to separate the two, but gently so, piercing the underbelly of the slate with caress and no venom.

It was the only beautiful sight Omsk had to offer.

The spires of the Ascension Cathedral and the Church of the Nicholas Cossack Troops, the domes and cupolas of the thirteen orthodox churches and the one mosque, many painted gold and others gay in ruby red and sapphire blue, gave the final touch to a Chinese artist's dream of 'Once Upon a Time'.

Yet somewhere in its middle was a prison where a man had rotted and emerged after four years hard labour to stir the world with "The House of the Dead". That man was Fedor Dostievsky.

The party wandered in and sought out the newspaper of the Omsk region, Akmolinsk, now known as The Akmolinsk Territory Gazette.

Boris tethered Poogavitsa and mounted the wooden steps. He asked to see the editor and mentioned the name of Sergei Alexandrovitch.

His path was cleared as if he was oil going through a machine.

"Where is Sergei Aledxandrovitch? And what's he

doing here? He ought to be in Moscow." A sturdy fifty year old had risen before Boris.

"He is below, injured, and asks to see you."

Radek grabbed his schuba and peaked cap.

"What happened to his friends?" the editor was asked.

"I should explain," offered Boris. "We are travelling companions of many months' standing, but we know nothing of each other's affairs. Perhaps you should not tell me. . ."

The editor smote Boris mightily and friendlily across the shoulder. "Touché!" he said. But Boris had never heard of the word.

Soon the six sledges were all inside an open yard which adjoined the office.

"There's a room on the other side. One minute." And Radek had gone.

He came back. "Yes. It's full of reams of paper and junk. I'll get some braziers in and warm it up. Let's not delay. No sense to take you home. We'll get a doctor here, and he'll tell us the best hospital. We want your leg better, Sergei, my man. God! what pain is in your eyes."

The sledge was separated from the animals. Two great doors were opened. In a trice a space was cleared and the sleigh pushed through by a score of hands and a shout.

The entire Buriat party were sent off with a journalist to the Shchepanov Hotel, and Boris was left alone with the Editor and Sergei.

"I want you to help my friend Boris to get some work for the winter. He's a good hunter," said Sergei.

"He can wait!" and Radek had given Boris another mighty crash across his shoulder blades. "Let the little to-be-hunted animals live another day, shall you, friend Boris? Sergei first. What say you?"

And a doctor came! Russia was not Russia any more!

80

Things never happened at this speed. Was Sergei the Czar of all the Russias in disguise?

37

Two gross, inflated outsize troikas left Zjennia's small township of Ch—— for the great city, the City of The Merchants, Samara.

The troikas were owned by Popovitch, Russia's foremost tea importer.

Uterus teeth had been discovered in Eva's womb, and the expected enquiry had been set afoot. Petchetkin, Samara's foremost specialist had been to Ch—— and reported that all was as it had been declared. He was returning with all the parties concerned to the city. In the front troika was Zjennia, Petchetkin and Eva, and in the second was Alexis, the priest, and Bogodin, Ch——'s only pretender to the office of doctor who, if pressed, could distinguish between a belch and a fart, but was lost when it came to analysing a hiccough.

Bogodin was also lost in the world of uterus teeth but promises of two crates of vodka had helped lessen his ignorance, and Alexis, as conversant seemingly in women's anatomy as he was in the affairs of the Church, seemed capable enough to carry the matter through.

The road dipped and a hundred feather-boarded, unpainted shacks at varying intervals registered the ending of Ch—— and the entering of the birch forest.

Though all Russia accepted cruelty as an ingredient of life, serfs expected it, prisoners got it, folk lore thrived on it and the cruelty makers, Ivan the Terrible, Peter the Great, Stenka Razin, Pugachev, became People's heroes,

Zjennia, whatever her feelings with the human species, was repelled at cruelty to animals. The troikas ran with the centre horse naturally, but with the outside horses having their necks twisted sideways outwards and if ever Popovitch sent her another carriage, it must never be a troika.

The thought spoilt the picture scene: the silver white of the birch, the magnolia white of the sky, the petrified white of the paths, and all the trees at attention like sentinels as the noble carriages threaded through.

Petchetkin did not stop talking. Zjennia had taken to him and wanted him alongside her on the ride. He was alive, bristling with tit-bits of knowledge, full of acquaintanceship with the famous and the infamous: but she soon realised that however meaty the matter, a non-stop talking machine with an 'I' in every sentence, is a tedium. And he was so loud! It was unfair to the birches in their winter slumber.

"I've been becoming an authority on uterus teeth for sometime," he was saying. "They were fortunate to find me now in Samara. They sent me to Olonetz, you must have heard?" Zjennia had neither heard of Olonetz nor Petchetkin, but the learned one didn't wait for an answer. "Yes, it has been going on for sixty years. The rumours, the innuendos. It's the Starovertzi sect, you know? It's forlorn there. A constant 40 under in the winter. The nuns and the monks. The inhabitants say they get together. The inhabitants say there is a great drowning of babies in the lake every July. The inhabitants say there'll have to be a new word for orgies. And there was to be this Committee of Enquiry, you must have heard? And I was specially sent from St. Petersburg. The inhabitants insisted that the lake be dredged. Such goings and comings in the horrific winter nights. And the macabre lakeside visitations in July. The nuns dress in long white, severely starched, highly

82

sheened cloth, so that you can see your reflections in them like mirrors: the sublimity of their dress is killing in its purity. Each figure seems furbished in saintliness. Then are the men equally sombrely and severely clad, in brilliant black. Indeed there are rooms where there are punishment utensils, if utensils is the word, where anyone tempted by the Devil might visit and exhort the Devil out of themself. And when you consider the pressures of the innuendos from the inhabitants the Devil must be always at their right hand."

"Did you find any babies?" Zjennia just squeezed in.

"That is the point. So gracious in their hospitality there, so extreme their desire to assist in our enquiries, that by the time all enquiries within were satisfied, ice had forced on the lakes and enquiries without had of necessity to be postponed until the next summer. Every delegation has hit on the same difficulty."

"But you had mentioned uterus teeth," Zjennia squeaked in again.

"Exactly! Exactly my dear child. Just what I was coming to. There seems that there was an epidemic there of womb disturbances. That is why St. Peterburg insisted I should be on the list for the Council of Enquiries. And I have seen with my very eyes such uterus teeth as would make your poor sister's seem ungrown. The growth is a defensive aberration, I say, a fear, where nature shows its ugly teeth – if you will forgive the pointed parallel. I am completing my thesis soon and must send it to the Czar's Academy of Medicine in St. Petersburg. That is why it is important to nip this epidemic in this Volga region in the bud."

So Eva was to become an epidemic?

The troika lumbered on like a sledge-hammer crushing crystals, and Petchetkin's voice lumbered heavier still, like a tom-tom crushing silence, and when the roly-poly-clad driver stopped to repair a rear strap,

Zjennia managed to effect the change so that Alexis made up their triumvirate in the front troika and "You two great masters in medicine must have the chance to share your knowledge and experience" in the second.

Alexis was a relief, but a problem too. He had presented Zjennia with a poem a day for a long time now and announced that this day's little something would bring the number to seventy. He read:

"'Honey hair and honey skin
Honey voice with poison in
Honey touch and laughter too
What must it be like being you?'

"Which of my seventy poems have you liked the best?"

"I haven't had the chance to read them all as yet, dear Alexis. Complete the hundred, my lover-priest, then I will bask in my century."

38

Hippolytus Popovitch, an oil and boil of a man, rose as a grotesque globule from an arm-chair to greet Zjennia. He had two pudge hams that served as hands, two bunches of bananas that served as fingers which managed to excrete some drops of stale moisture on to her palms. He followed this up by a slobber from an orifice which reminded Zjennia of a bum she had seen on the backside of a mandrille which however served Hippolytus as a mouth, and that too left some runny excrescences on her hand. And then the puffing polyp of a merchant sank back into his oversized arm-chair letting himself go like a tired thick rubber balloon, till all his fat, fit, and chair and Popovitch became once more united into one coagulated mass.

"Sit where you care, my dear Yevgennia. I have forty servants in my house and they are all at your command. Use them as you will."

The Enquiry had gone the way the representatives of Ch—— had wished; and Petchetkin had been a god-send to their cause. Eva had already left with Bogodin and Alexis for Ch——, unable to wait a moment to get the good news to Nikolai, the shy schoolmaster on whose innocent behalf this whole charade had been played out.

When Zjennia heard that the assembly of would-be wedding gifts were to arrive in Samara that evening, and that silks and sables were among them, she agreed to accept the hospitality of Popovitch for the night.

"So sorry, my dear Yevgennia," the globule was saying, "that I am a merchant in tea. What can there be in tea to appeal to ravishing young things like yourself? Money I have and money I can give, but there are so many other products of trade that might have brought me the appeals of, of. . . of ravishing young things."

Popovitch rang a bell he kept by his chair.

A giant appeared. "Umar, bring the young lady a foot-stool."

One glance at Umar and something stirred in Zjennia's centre-point.

The man left for a foot-stool. "He's a Tartar. One of my head servants," Popovitch heaved the words out.

A Tartar? A giant? A man like. . . like. . . Zjennia felt like thinking 'Boris', but she would not let herself. And a servant too. Now placing the footstool under her feet.

"Take my boots off," she said. He did so. "You can place my feet back on the stool. Your name is Umar? You have a wife, Umar?"

"No madame."

"But you are thirty?"

"No madame, twenty-five."

"Bring the stool a little nearer! Umar, you'll show me round the master's house a little later."

"Yes madame."

Forty servants there were, and probably forty rooms as well. A square house: solid, unpretentious outside, overloaded with fat, bulbous furniture inside, gross comfort oozing everywhere. 'I like the smell of riches,' thought Zjennia. 'I like the smell of forty servants. And one in particular. And I like the view from the window of the sprawling Volga, two miles of it at least.'

The centre of Samara was built on the high cliffs which cradled the great curve eastwards of the Volga one mile wide beneath them. Ships were everywhere, some of them the largest in the world.

Samara was townish, not cityish: it was solid, not flamboyant; it was elegant but not showy; its mentality was of merchants and traders: it had three theatres but that's only because any Russian town of such a size had three theatres; and the theatres were always full but that was only because the people had to have somewhere to show themselves. Samara had a Cathedral with thirteen gilt domes, and many a fine church with Voznesenie as its gem: but that was only because the merchants wanted God on their side. The air was of honest respectability and such bent practices as it had were kept for business where they were seen as business and not as bent practices.

Zjennia yearned for a larger world than Ch—— and that flabby-as-a-sponge jellyfish Popovitch, with two beads as eyes, set her thinking. He was so revolting, he appealed to the lavatory side of her lust, she could think of nothing snugger than getting curled up among those whales of flesh. Since the departure of Boris, the more she stood in need of sex the cruder she fancied it.

Dear porpoise Popovitch did not know what he had let into his den. Or did he?

A Chinese merchant called. It was the merchant who had brought the wedding gifts. But the goods had remained on the quayside and still had to be delivered.

"Ring for Umar," Zjennia said. And Popovitch did so. She had never had servants to treat as minions before. And she loved that too!

"Prepare the couch by the window, Umar," she said. "I want to rest. Make it comfortable."

So she stayed in the room while the two merchants talked. She did not mean to listen, but she did.

The Chinaman wondered how to get gold into China? Zjennia thought the commerce had been tea?

"The Harbin Syndicate would find gold invaluable. It's the only article the Czarist Government will not allow to be exported. But that trebles its value if we could get it through."

"Dead bodies," wheezed Popovitch. "That's the answer." He gurgled, which for him was laughing. "All Chinamen in Russia should discover a wish to be buried in the land of their forbears. We'll take six months to whip up the fervour. Such a national spirit ought to be encouraged. You bring your train of waggons of tea bricks here. You fill the empty waggons with Chinese bodies to return. At Irkutsk, before the border, we stop your waggon train to add more salt to preserve the poor deceased, then blow gold dust up their nostrils, mouths, ears, and other entrances" – guffaws – "You can carry a lot of gold dust in our exits and our entrances –" a guggle from Popovitch and a giggle from the Chinaman – "We unload mainly at Harbin. Get me a list of fifty towns around Harbin and we will discover that most of our Russo-Chinese hailed from there. . ."

Another roar from one and more tinny wheezes from the other and three quick downed vodkas, came with the thought.

"Hippolytus," said the Chinaman carefully. "They've discovered it's cheaper to send the tea direct by ship from Canton to St. Petersburg rather than by this long tedious land route via Samara."

"Of course it is. But tea tastes best that has traversed deserts. Tea should only travel overland."

"Hippolytus," the Chinaman whispered. "You and I know that it makes no difference."

"You and I are the only two in the world who know that it doesn't! All St. Petersburg, Moscow, Kazan and the Almighty Czar himself are convinced that it does." They downed three more vodkas still. "Besides, tell them it would be sad to see the gold dust taking the golden road to Samarkand when it could be taking the Silk road to China."

And Umar was there.

"The cargo has been delivered, sir."

"Praise be! Zjennia, my dearest sweetest Zjennia. Where shall we see the cargo? Here? Or in your room?"

"My room?"

"Yes, your room Yevgennia. You've always had a room here."

"I'll see it in my room."

What mystery was in this?

39

Umar took Zjennia to the top room in the house. He seemed to know exactly where to go. And he seemed to know it as her room.

It was a spacious room with windows on all sides and a vast view from one of them of the Mother River. It was beautifully, if over, furnished. The thirteen gilt domes of the Cathedral of Our Lady of Kazan were glorified in the light of the fresh winter sun. Two tables had bulbous legs. A Fujiyama screen led on to an elaborately carved wardrobe. The Uzbek carpets were thick. The bed. . . that's what Zjennia adored: the bed of a Czarina, on a dais two steps high, with heavy curtainings round. Was she dreaming? Her room?

Servants were bringing up the merchandise. Forty servants to order about. Strange feelings were growing in her. Wealth: so it means something? And here was Umar helping the others. Such dignity in Umar. And the fire of the Tartar flashed in his eyes.

"How long has this been my room, Umar?"

"Since the day the master's son became engaged to your sister, madame."

"And Eva? She has a room here, Umar?"

"That is one floor down."

"As fine as this?"

"Not so large, madame."

"And where is the master's wife?"

"She has a wing of her own. Three rooms."

Popovitch had married his wife to get the quayside her father owned. But having provided her with one son, he considered he had fulfilled his obligations.

Popovitch rolled into the room, though it was not the vodka that made him roll – vodka affected him no more than tea affected others – a roll and a wobble were his natural gaits.

Old grey rag bundles were unravelled.

Zjennia marched over and saw a silk softer than rose petals, softer than snow. She rested it against her face. It beguiled her.

"From China?"

"From Pekin."

"And this? And this? And this?" She was bewitched.

89

Then a bull's hide appeared. Black, tough as hell, enormous, why did it make her think of Boris? She did not want to think of Boris. Nothing in her life ever overwhelmed her, ever seduced her, as the sight of that bull's hide.

"From China?"

"From the annual fair at Tobolsk."

"Wedding gifts?" Zjennia asked.

Popovitch was in a mesmeric trance. "For you," he said.

"Wedding gifts?"

"For this room. For you," he said.

Zjennia went to him and, hands on hips, said "For Eva!"

"For you."

"Umar, leave us," asked Zjennia. The Tartar left.

"The marriage was for Eva!" she said, her hazel green eyes as hard as emeralds.

"For you. Oh God!"

And a pin burned in the emeralds. "So it's Oh God, is it? Your son was to marry Eva!"

"Yes. Then they would live here. And you would visit us."

"Would I?"

He crumpled in a heap at her feet. He was in tears. "For you," he said again.

"Did your son love Eva?"

"No."

"No?"

"He has his love in town."

"And he was to marry Eva?"

"For half my business."

Popovitch was pitiful. A grumous toad at her feet.

"And he would have loved Eva?"

"Only as I have loved my wife. He had his love in the city."

"Get up and sit over there!"

He struggled to do so.

"I?"

"I worship you. Every year you come to Samara Fair and I see you from the distance. I gave half my world to have you near me. I'd give the other half. . . that bloody fool, Petchetkin! You and I know there is no such thing as uterus teeth! But the young things both wanted the way out and you and that pompous ass Petchetkin gave it them."

He rolled in an upwards direction and came and collapsed in a heap at her feet again.

"Get up!! If you do that again, I'll leave by the instant and Umar will drive me through the night to Ch——. Get back to your chair!"

He did so.

"You were willing to ruin my sister. . ."

"No."

"Yes!"

"What was I to do?"

"You will pack up all these gifts. The bull's-hide you will send to the finest tailor in Samara and he will make a dress for me. All else, the three diamonds, the three topaz, you have Umar take to Eva, hoping that she will recover from her illness and be lucky at some time to find the swain of her heart, and, hoping so, here are her first wedding gifts. Three other things. Firstly, you will never send me a troika again. You will send only a one person sledge with one horse. Secondly, you are only ever to send Umar out to Ch——. If you ever appear yourself there, I will never see you again. Thirdly. Tonight I will sleep with the biggest cheat in Samara."

His beady eyes looked up and lit like lost stars.

"But not if you grovel at my feet!"

40

First, there was the feast. Forty servants went about in forty circles, bringing forty dishes, running up and down four wide staircases.

Then between bouts of lusting, Zjennia nestled into the folds and mesh-mash of this excrescence and listened to his stories:

"The king of the jungle said 'I am the king of the jungle, the next two animals I meet must make love to each other.' The first was a giraffe and the second a mouse. And the king issued his commands. After one hour, all things seeming too quiet, the king went in search of his subjects, and found the mouse panting around the neck of the giraffe, half dead. 'How is this?' asked the king. 'What with kissing at one end,' panted the mouse, 'and fun and games at the other, I must have covered five miles in the hour since you left us.'"

"A hunter, lost in the Silver Wood near Moscow, was about to put his foot down, when a little daisy cried out 'Don't put your foot down. Then I can grant you three wishes, any three wishes you like. Only you must remember your vilest enemy shall get twice the wish that you get.' The hunter said 'I will have a palace carved from gold, with all furnishings fashioned from silver.' 'That I can give,' said the daisy, 'only remember your vilest enemy will get twice of your one palace. What is your second wish?' 'The thousand most beautiful girls in the world.' 'Yes, I can grant that also. Only remember your most cunning enemy will receive two thousand. What is your third wish?' 'I will have one bollock removed.'"

41

Elk had appeared in the few woods round Omsk. The hunting community was excited and planned immediate action.

A group of nine had been formed, seven Buriats and two Russians, and all had sworn a quantity of oaths for their mutual good. The Editor, Radek, asked them to include Boris. The Buriats refused. Nine was their number and the gods would plot against them if they took more. Then someone pointed out that nine was the hunting number but someone had to remain with the sledge teams while the hunt was on. So Boris went along as minder. And he obliged with some oaths he did not understand, to gods he had never heard of, who, he learned, would be burnt – the gods – if the hunt was not successful and new gods put in their places. Boris also understood that his schuba and ice-shoes would have to be destroyed if the hunt failed and new ones worn next time.

Three dog teams were hired from a merchant and the group set out at five in the morning. The three dog teams seemed only interested in tearing each other apart, and searched for any sniff of a chance to do so.

There was a birch wood north of Omsk and another in the south and the hunters drove north.

A Buriat developed violent stomach agonies and Boris was told he would deputise for the hunt, stomach pains evidently not preventing a man who could not hunt from keeping three sets of six dogs from tearing each other asunder.

Boris had taken the precaution, in case he'd be called upon, of marking his bullets, he being told that it was the habit to remove any bullets from any animal hit, and the owners of the bullets shared the winnings.

And what had Boris done? He had marked his bullets with ')H('* Why? A funny sort of compulsion had come over him. He smiled it off 'Let her have the credit. Go bullet and capture her a skin she will be mad about. Will she bring me luck? I hope so.' He smiled it off, yes; but felt a twist like a catch compel his hand.

The nine set off to form an immense circle: eight walking two hundred paces on their sliding shoes, then seven two hundred more, then six two hundred more, and so forth.

Then they all moved forward diminishing the circle till they met in the middle — and no elk. The gods had not honoured their pleas, no doubt having taken a dislike to Boris. The nine had met up in a clearing. And no smile.

So the sledges left for another area. Someone spotted hoof marks: the spirits soared: and the gods seemed having second thoughts about Boris. Four elk passed them like a silent wind before the circle had even begun to form.

The second venture brought one success. The circle closed in until the elk made a bid for escape: then all shot. Boris wondered what would happen if they missed the elk and hit each other: but later learned he had already sworn that if he was the owner of a bullet removed from a man instead of an animal he should be shot himself if he had not effected his exit from Omsk within twenty-four hours.

Boris had hit the elk. And two others had as well.

The giant elk had found suddenly its front legs could

*)H(for Zjennia

94

not spring and it had crashed horribly over its own antlers.

Three elk were caught that first day. Twelve white hares, twenty ducks and two beavers. It was found that Boris had hit each elk, and in exactly the same spot, just above the heart. This fact was bandied around and it was agreed that it was obvious that it was the gods who had hit the seventh Buriat below his solar plexus and let in Boris.

In town Boris walked to the Zaitsev Hotel with one of the Russian hunters, Anton, where they both lodged. They were passing the grandest building in town, the Ascension Cathedral, when everything came to a halt. Room was needed for three hundred prisoners. Halters at their necks, manacles at their wrists, ball-chains on their feet. More forlorn than skeletons, more haggard than slain men. Not one upright, and not one with a decent coat! In fifteen degrees below zero. What did God think from the Ascension Cathedral? Anton said: "They are from the Trans-Siberian Railway station and have another mile or two to the Cossack Village to the north." Omsk was divided into nine villages, and the Cossacks held sway only over the one named simply 'Cossack Village'.

Boris said to himself: 'The worst thing I ever did was not to explain to Zjennia why I did what I did on our wedding night. The best thing I ever did was to escape from Samara jail before. . .' and he looked at the last few convicts as they dragged themselves forward.

Anton continued: "I worked in an office here in Omsk that issued 100,000 schubas and 100,000 jerkins to convicts. I only counted 20,000. The remainder got lost among the manufacturers' families and the inspectors and staff on the way. Even I got one. But 100,000 were signed for. The Czar pays for each convict. How much reaches each convict? Someone told this to the Czar. He said: 'I do my duty. I leave it to others to do theirs.' These here will either end in the coal-mines at Zaisan or in the gold-mines at Marka-Kul. One tenth of what they mine goes to the Czar. Two tenths goes to the tax collectors, nearly always Cossacks. One tenth of the furs and skins you hunt goes to the Czar. But he gave us the Cathedral didn't he? Fortunately we are outside Cossack jurisdiction here but we also give one tenth to the merchant who hired us the sledges and one tenth to the Governor of Siberia who lives in the only stone building down this street."

In his hotel room Boris took out his remaining bullets and saw the ')H(' on each. 'What game is yours, Zjennia? Are you always going to bring me luck? Or was it the hides you were after? We'll have to stick to the ")H(" now, won't we? Can't turn away from such omens, can we?' And then he marked more. And kissed the lot.

42

"Sergei," said Boris, "one of hunting group is a Russian, Anton, from Saratov. He wants to come to see you?"

Sergei was more at peace now. He had not broken his hip-bone but seriously fractured it. The doctors had done all they could and it was mending.

"Anton? I know him. Bring him along. So."

The grimmest thing about that hospital was the lack of lights, a few mean candles, and most of them trying hard not to burn. The cleverest thing was that some great man had insisted on treble glazed windows and treble doors, so that the neverending howl of the winds across and through the highways and byways of this one-storey-ed town – there were thirty buildings only of more than one storey and only twelve of them of stone, the rest being all timber – these gusts from the teeth of the icy north were kept to the outside world, and, more important, the cold was kept out.

Anton met Boris next noon in the hotel lobby. Boris could never fathom whether Anton was just getting into his clothes or getting out of them: at his neatest he looked like an unmade bed with trousers tumbling around his ankles like waterfalls. For this special visit to the hospital he had put on a collar which had to fight to retain its place about his neck.

Anton changed character as he met Sergei. He became obsequious. So who and what was Sergei?

Anton undid an untidy packet and took out a carving and it seemed it was a gift for the sick man.

"You see, I got this piece of antler horn, and carved about it with a knife, and I have rubbed in black charcoal and evened it off. Do you think Alicia will like it?"

"Alicia?" asked Sergei. "Alicia will be very proud. That is fine work. Be proud, Anton. So." Then it was not for the sick man.

"Who is Alicia?" asked Boris.

"Oh my wife, of course, no one else. Sergei has visited her in Saratov and seen my two fine boys too."

Anton was perhaps more proud to display his prowess before Sergei, than to send it to his wife. "Boris here, is going to help me post it, aren't you Boris?"

"If you say so, Anton."

"It's very beautiful craftsmanship," said Sergei. "You did it with slow care, too. Always tackle a craft slowly, Anton. So."

"I could do a little piece for you," said Anton.

"So. Do that," said Sergei. "Volkov has a small factory for ornaments and trinkets. Uh. You might like to work there. I could speak to him. Think about it, Anton."

Boris had never sent a parcel anywhere in his life. He was entirely unprepared for the palaver that followed.

There were six queues to be faced and all were long. And the oddest thing about the queues was that they criss-crossed, so, watch-out, else you'd get caught wrong, like in snakes-and-ladders.

The first queue was for paper and string. "Why did you not make the parcel up at the hotel?" "They prefer it this way," said Anton. "Then they can know what's in it, and what they are sending. Actually, also, no one knows in Omsk where you can buy string and. . . you see that man over there?" He pointed to a bewildered bearded young man. "He's been sent away to iron his paper out. He was asked, what would his friends think of Omsk if they allowed such a disgraceful packet through their mail?" The next queue was the queue for collecting the packet, now packed. Then a third queue for it to be weighed. Each time a slip was issued, this one, telling the weight of the parcel. Then the fourth queue for telling the cost of the stamp for such a weight. Then a queue to buy the stamp itself. Then a queue for a receipt for posting it.*

Then if Anton and Omsk were lucky the parcel would just arrive at its destination with a last gasp of string left and a fraction sample of Omsk paper.

Boris soon realised why he had been asked to come along. While Anton stood in the first queue, he stood in the second. When Anton was served he came like a long lost friend to chat away the time of day with Boris. When the queue had got used to their presence, Boris slunk away and joined the third queue. Only once were they in trouble for their queue jumping act, then Anton explained that Boris was General Voronovsky in civilian clothes and should be allowed to hurry,

*Such practices still persist in many parts to this day — Author's note

98

whereupon a small pinched man three behind said he was the Czar's nephew and all the queue discovered they were V.I.P.s in a hurry – but the friends had already passed on, leaving the queue they had deserted to argue out their greatnesses.

Two hours to send one parcel and Anton thanked Boris for helping him knock off one hour from the usual wait: "You have to go early," he said. "At six o'clock they slam all windows down and it's up your mother's ass if you are the next in the last queue of the whole bloody game, you just have to come back next day."

43

At the hotel they were in for another Old Russian Custom. The long, long wait for the restaurant meal.

Boris met a man who said he had once received a meal before one hour was up. No one believed him and Boris didn't. No one wanted to believe him. A five hundred year tradition becomes sacred and no one feels at ease to hear of its being broken. The Czar was busy in these years with setting up Committees of Enquiry and it would be a curiosity to know what happened between the issuing of an order for a meal and the delivering of it. Perhaps to know that though would spoil the wait which had become a way of life.

"It might be like knowing what happens after death," agreed Anton. "Sometimes it's best to leave things unknown."

They, Anton and Boris, for the moment had vodka and kumyss before them and so settled down to the oldest Siberian custom of all, the Savouring of the Passing of Time.

"How did Sergei meet your wife and children?" asked Boris.

And Anton, his ebullient self once again, said: "Ha good old Boris, good friend Boris, let me tell you.

"I came down here on a ten year sentence. Half of us did, eh? And I was sent to the gold mines. There, if you survive two winters, you survive. When my sentence finished, listen to this, Boris my boy, Boris my good comrade, you won't believe this! Ha!' He was laughing so much his clothes snaked about him like pools of snakes all over his chair. "I went to see this fellow, this governor, who told me I was being released, and outside, as I left his office there was this tiny passage filled up with this iron trolley thing and in this trolly thing 'V' shaped trays of tiny gold nuggets. I grabbed five, rushed to the toilet, and jabbed four of them up my ass. I swallowed the smallest, the fifth. I reckoned I could shit them all out next day and come out rich. And bugger them for their ten years hard! But I got jammed up: I got the shits in my heart frightened I couldn't shit in my ass. The Holy Mary save me I was bloody buggered well near for another ten years! I thought I'd never get out of that prison. Then when I was out next day I straight away panicked and dashed to the hospital. Here, listen to this, Boris my boy, Boris my comrade, you won't believe this! Ha! That bloody gold wouldn't come out. One perishing chunk blocked the whole bleeding passage." Anton was revelling in it now. "But oh no! not then. And me so near with this blessing for my dear Alicia!" He rolled about all over his chair like a roller-coaster.

"Came to this same bloody hospital as dear old Sergei is at now. And! Cripes, it's true, my dear friend Boris! what saved me! – God help me, it's true! Sergei saved

100

me! I had told those bloody people what I had done and like a flame half of Omsk seemed to turn up demanding my gold. Nephews, nieces, sons, best friends: none of whom I'd ever heard of: and the bloody doctors themselves had designs on my golden rear. And dear old Sergei, dear old Sergei, he was visiting a comrade, he came and whispered 'I'm your long lost father, Anton my boy, I'll see you right in this.' And he winked at me. And everyone was disgusted. They believed him! They saw their claims receding and they bloody nearly didn't operate. No interest. But curiosity beat them in the end. And Sergei beat them. And four of the bleeding pieces came out. And to this day no one knows what's happened to the fifth. Boris, my boy, dear ol' son, you might be sitting opposite a gold mine! D'you know they even stuck a magnet up? Old Sergei made sure I got my bleedin' gold. The only gold ever mined out of shit."

"Where is it now?"

"In the vaults of the State Siberian Bank awaiting the arrival of dear Alicia."

"I'll tell you what you are doing with the fifth nugget," said Boris.

"And that, my friend?"

"You are keeping it in safest custody for the Czar of all the Russias. His ten per cent."

Anton rolled on the floor.

Then he got up. "If it comes out," he asked, "will you, Boris my boy, help me post it from the Omsk Post Office? We'll clean it first. Must show respect."

Boris said: "I don't trust them at that Post Office, Anton! Best keep it where it's safe, just for now."

Anton whispered: "Shall we let Alicia have a look for it?"

"That would be a real test!" said Boris. "You could find a lot out about a wife with a Test like that!"

And the borsch came.

101

"And the Incumbents of the Omsk Area of the South Siberian Syndicate for the all-embracing Rights of Czarist Settlers!" said Anton.

44

Anton shouted across the room to six rotund merchants who had just arrived – merchants in prisoners.

They all shared a table. But not the vodka: the Syndicate ordered their own. In bottles.

"Why in bottles?" asked Boris.

A man with even a fourth jowl to his face, like a pudgy bull-dog, put his arm round Boris, pounded him lightly in the stomach and explained:

"Never order in glasses! You pay for the first glass. The second pays for itself. The third is diluted and the fourth only smells right. These buggers have four grades of vodka according to the state you're in. Don't be a sucker. Get it right from the start. Order in bottles." And another dig in the ribs helped make the point.

"Do you know any escaped prisoners who would like to be sent home? Anton has helped us with many." And another pummel in the ribs.

"How?" asked Boris.

"We send escaped prisoners home. We pay them well. People don't know their rights. We know them. And we know the best prices. We 'catch' escaped prisoners – those who want to get away from it all for the winter – we put them aboard the puff-puff. Home sends them back out again. We usually get the time extended till the spring. The government pay to have 'caught' escapees, and pay again to have them transported back. We share the payments with the prisoners. If they can they bring back their families with them, then the Czar gives each one a hundred roubles. We share that too. Some make a regular thing of it every winter."

"Do they ever get home?"

"Nope." Another punch in the ribs. "They know the rules. We know the finances. Stopped by their province. The militia get their cut for sending them back. We help everybody. One fellow we have never stops travelling: he's permanently being re-habilitated. Knows the world backwards he does. Does well. Likes travelling."

The whole party ordered tea as well as vodka. They drank their tea through sugar cubes they held between their clenched teeth. Then they spat what remained of the cube back into a common bowl and picked up anyone's half finished cube for their next glass.

"Of course we like groups. Put us on to a group — Boris, isn't it? — yes, Boris, put us on to a group and you'll get your cut too. Everyone wins with us. Ask Anton. We deal with migrants too. Joachim there, third from the left, he got 5000 Old Believers from Rumania settled near the Amur three years ago. Czar happy, Rumania happy, Old Believers happy. We are the happiest bunch of do-good fiddlers in the continent. Ask Anton. Always happy. Everyone wins, that's our motto. We moved the Rumanians on from the Amur to the Ussuri. Better for them. They got paid again: we got paid again. Know the rules. Here's a secret."

He bent close to Boris's ear: Christ! what a loathsome breath! "I help gypsies. People have never done right by gypsies. The world over talks of freedoms and liberties. The gypsies should be our gods. Can't chain a gypsy. I'd sell my soul for a gypsy. They are the torch-bearers and no one recognises it. Except old Petrov here, that's me. And their women! Pheel! Some of them Rumanians and

Hungarians were gypsies that got mixed in like. Pheel! A thousand Raskolnikovs wanted to be rehabilitated to St. Petersburg. Can't do that. They have to migrate before they can rehabilitate. So migrated them to Omsk and after a year to St. Petersburg. Good payments, Boris, friend of Anton. Did you hear of Anton's golden ass?" And Patrov splattered his tea, half sugar cube, vodka and all over Boris, pummelling his ribs meanwhile, till Boris managed to return his attention to his fellow hunter, Anton, as the Beef Stroganoff arrived.

"You never told me, Anton," said Boris, "how Sergei came to meet your wife."

"Ah! Ha! Ha! that was the whole thing. You see, Boris my boy, Boris old comrade, when we met up in that hospital we already had known each other. It was some six years previous to that that I was on a transfer. He was on a visit. We got talking at a Railway Halt. He saw me, chained I was. And he came and talked on the bench I was chained to. I told him. You see, convicts' wives have a free divorce if they want it," – Boris worried to learn that – "Alicia said Never, she'd wait for me. Always. She will. They would have paid her to come here, children too. And I could have worked in the prison, in the mine, and been at home each night. Sergei offered to see her. He had to go to Saratov for some reason of his own. He came back and said like this: if she waited and brought the kids when the sentence was over, there'd be a lot more pride to it and we could build a grand real life and no shadows round us. She's coming next summer. The Syndicate have fixed it. Kids too. She's right. And Sergei's right. Pride, you know. We'll be free. With pride. It's been a long wait. Ten years! Sergei said 'She's a one-man woman, Anton, have no other thoughts.' And that she is. And I am a one-woman man, Boris, my boy, I swear to it! Have no other thoughts! Howling winds and bitter cold: Omsk is grim,

104

Boris. But there's freedom here, Boris. Not in Saratov. I've done my sentence. I'm FREE. And when you have pride, Boris, free, with pride, Boris. . ."

Boris put his arm round him. "And you have kept all your gold for Alicia!"

Anton put his arm round Boris and whispered back: "It's in the bank, Boris! The State Bank of Siberia, Boris!"

"To Alicia, Anton!" And Boris rose up to his great height.

"To Alicia, Boris!" And Anton stood small beside him.

And they drank to that.

And broke their glasses.

"And to what you have *secreted* for her!" said Boris softly.

"*In* my secret bank?"

"*Up* your secret bank!"

And they drank to that too.

And broke their glasses again.

As all good Russians should.

45

One hunt was a bow and arrow affair. On a morning when the wind played taciturn, merely crying in a sobbing sound, yet, in fact so flashing a hundred little ice needles against the face as to pare the skin, on such a morning the Buriats led the hunt party out to bushes, shrubs or trees and affixed arrows heavily loaded at their heads with hay or wheat. Hidden behind each arrow was a trap that, as the hay was touched, released the arrow with such viciousness as to kill any deer or game that had touched the hay.

Then the party was led away to the few streams still uncovered by ice and on to an unfrozen gully where the tributary Om joined the mighty Irtush – 3000 miles long, it could stretch from England to America – and the Buriats taught all how to arrow fish: stirlet, sturgeon, trout or nelma.

It was a Buriat's god's day. All had had to pray before the god's idol, had had to feed a fire before it – the Buriats had had to dance too. All had sworn to beat the god to pulp if there was no success, or to buy him new clothes and burn him a thousand tallow candles if the catches proved of worth.

The god won, and the haul was joyous. With Boris the hero and elected as half-Ongon (half-god) so Boris hoped that wouldn't mean he'd be beaten to a half-pulp if the next hunt failed.

The Buriats had proudly supplied all the arrows which had had heavy, fat heads, with a point less than half a thumb long. The Buriats explained the necessity for the heavy heads, but Boris had never yet understood anything any Buriat had ever explained to him and neither did he understand this.

The only time the Buriats allowed a gun – it was their day and their god was a pre-gun god – was when they needed to rest a man-height pole into the ground and they made a hole by shooting bullets into the frozen surface until they had one the right size.

To the dancing delight of the Buriats a deer was shot by a hay-arrow on the hunters' first return to the spot.

All agreed it was a mighty god they were worshipping and it would be a sumptuous outfit of clothes the god's idol would be getting. The greatest gifts were amulets, a deerskin cap and a shirt of bear's ear, but as there were no bears this far south they would have to settle for a

second-hand bear's ear bought by their half-Ongon,
Boris himself.

46

      "I want you to help in a Court case the
day after tomorrow," said Sergei.
    "A Court case?"
    "You remember Vassili?"
    "Of course."
    "He's been arrested. So."
    "He's in Omsk?"
    "Uh. Didn't you know? He never went home with the
others. He got a job in Kornikov's home."
    "Who's Kornikov?"
    "General Kornikov is the recently appointed Military
Governor of the Akmolinsk Territory. He has one of the
very few stone houses here and Vassili had become one
of the twenty servants."
    "And Vassili?"
    "Is accused of stealing from him."
    "And you?"
    "I speak Russian. Vassili pretends he doesn't. So,
shall we say, I'm the interpreter? You better pretend too
– pretend you don't know him. A wink, maybe. He'd
like that. So."
    "And me?"
    "I will be taken there in a wheel bed. The bed enables
me to sit up. But I want you at my side. If I don't speak
loud enough you will convey my words on to the Court.
But, mostly, keep your eye on Kornikov. The entrance to
the court is the only exit and is near the front where the

judges and ourselves are placed. Under no circumstances let Kornikov get away under any pretence he will make. Bar his way at the exit. Let no one out after the proceedings have begun. Be a massive one-man shut-door."

47

When Boris arrived at the court it was already full. The case was being covered by all four newspapers.

The new Governor, who had already made a firm mark on the authorities in Omsk, had apprehended the thief in a startling fashion that he would divulge in Court.

There was much jockeying for seats. The benches were full and the floor spaces were full. The fact that Sergei was speaking for Vassili had been hinted at but not confirmed.

The bed with Sergei was wheeled in among whisperings of approval. The judge appeared and the case was on its way with a mere hour's delay. Boris had measured his stretch across the door and he could hold it within his two wide arms. But for the moment he stood by Sergei's side. He bent down to listen to Sergei. Sergei whispered: "Vassili is only speaking Buriat," and he winked. "Don't forget. So."

Kornikov was as erect as a lamp-post, and twice as broad. He was a supreme example of a military man. He began apologising for his not being in his Akmolinsk uniform but that he felt that the present case was a local one and out of respect for the court he was appearing in his Omsk dress. Indeed, he was very resplendent. His uniform was the finest piece of theatre any present had seen. His medals glittered and brought sparkle into a drab area. Some there were in indecisive blacks fast relapsing into shoddy greys, most were in tired browns, and the nearest that came to a describable colour was an ex-official in brown gravy.

He, Kornikov, General Nikolai Ivanovitch Kornikov, had discovered to his dismay that the centre piece of a family heirloom, a work of mesmeric art in sapphire, ruby and gold, had been missing. He had questioned all his twenty staff separately and together but had learned nothing. After enquiries at the Bank where he had recently declared the treasure, and after soul-searching questioning and seeking advice from close friends, and after trying ruses and setting traps to no avail, he had hit on an ingenious plan for discovering the thief. He had owed it to his wife to do so for she, poor soul, was distraught at the loss. He half owed it too, perhaps the Court would forgive him for saying so, indeed to himself to apprehend the thief.

There were eight servants who had had access to the place where the heirloom was kept. He had called them all in and stood them all before a long table. On the table he had placed eight glasses. In the glasses he had poured water. Into each he had dropped a pellet – a pellet evolved from black bread. It would sink slowly. It might even take two minutes to sink to the bottom. If the guilty man among them owned up before the pellet touched the bottom he would be dealt with leniently, if the guilty man failed to do so he would be dealt with with all the harshness his, Kornikov's, conscience could grant. The prisoner-in-the-dock had owned to the theft in the last seconds as the pellet touched bottom.

The General expected and got a hum of approval from the whole court, even, from one section, a most unusual applause, which the judge thought he should discourage, but did not. After all, this man was in line to become the next Governor of Omsk as well as of the County of Akmolinsk.

The greatly satisfied General sat down on a stool thrust before him, which he was at pains to show thanks for, but he was immediately on his feet again.

"I could have dealt with the case myself in my own authority but saw it more my duty to bring the case to the Court where, I must hasten to add, the culprit having admitted the crime, should be served a milder sentence than otherwise, especially as I had promised all eight that that should be the case."

Another hum of approval. And a little more applause.

Sergei wanted to say something. Boris repeated louder that Sergei was requesting the prisoner to speak in self-defence.

Vassili, looking hopelessly down with eyes even more riveted to the floor than he had ever had before, began, Sergei repeating sentence by sentence loudly in Russian.

"Huragin was given his father's bones so that he could piece them together before burying them. All was there except the great toe of his right foot. Huragin searched everywhere till he found the trail of Ungin, the fox, who had stolen the toe. But he followed the trail further and discovered that Ungin had been eaten by Shono, the wolf. Going still farther he found that Shono had been devoured by Hara Grojung, the black bear. Yet still further on he found that Hara Grojung had been devoured by Bara, the tiger. But Bara himself had been eaten by Irbit, the lion. Huragin killed Irbit and inside his stomach found his father's big toe which fitted the foot exactly. Huragin sprinkled his father's skeleton with healing water and then with the Water of Life and then mixed in powdered bark from the red restoring

110

larch trees. Then flesh came to the bones, then sleep to the prostrate form, then the father was well and lived."

There were murmurings, and bewilderment on the face of the judge, and ridicule on the face of the General as if pointing out that they were dealing with an out-of-mind simpleton.

Sergei motioned to Boris. Boris knew what he had to do, and while Sergei apologised to the judge for temporarily borrowing the front portion of his long table, Boris laid out eight glasses and brought in a jug of water.

The General jumped up. "This is not necessary. The experiment was made at my home and came out conclusive."

Sergei said: "General Kornikov, we do not doubt your experiment in the least and we do not dispute it. The Court may take note that I do not dispute your experiment, or your findings. Indeed we accept them. This, General, is purely my own experiment. Bring on the servants." And Boris ushered seven men forward — eight with the prisoner.

Kornikov, a little put out, said sharply: "These are not the same men!"

"Which are not the same men?"

"The third and the fifth. They are not the same men."

"We have the others near at hand. They are guarding your carriage. But does it matter? This concerns one man, doesn't it, the prisoner in the dock?"

The General made a blowing action with his lips and a stomping with his foot. "I suppose not. But hurry on my man. I have pressing work at the Military Office and cannot stay long. I only came to present my case. The man has confessed. You and everyone have accepted it. So can we get through this Christmas charade quickly?"

"Certainly. Put another glass please." Boris did so. "To help us through in utmost speed, General, perhaps you'll accept the ninth glass and you can tell us how to proceed?"

"I won't take part! What insult is this! I'm not on trial!" And he laughed and there was a faint sympathetic laugh or two from the court.

"Is this necessary?" asked the judge.

Sergei said: "It would expedite the Experiment exceedingly. The General has pressing business he wants to attend to. This Court, I am sure, has a busy pile up of cases to attend to, and after all, the General has nothing to fear since a man cannot steal from himself, can he? His role is simply to expedite the proceedings."

"Please sit in," said the judge.

"I will not!!" bawled the General which shook the court. Why such vehemence?

"Perhaps the guard would put in the water."

Boris presumed he was the guard, and filled each glass.

"Perhaps the guard would let the pellets drop? Oh, see if the General approves of the pellets first."

And Boris shoved the pellets under the fuming General's eyes. Kornikov made a sort of grunt, which was a little like a 'Mmm' so that was taken as an acceptance.

"Perhaps the guard will drop the pellets in?" said Sergei from his pillows.

Boris went first to the General's glass. Kornikov was up in a second and sent the glass flying, with all the water. "I told you to leave me out of this! The indignity of asking an injured party to take part in a test of guilt!"

Boris had recovered the glass and quietly re-filled it.

"I told you! . . ." roared the General.

Boris had been alert and put his body between the huge General and the small glass this time. And it was noted that Boris's frame matched that of the General. Perhaps even one inch taller. And every bit as fine a figure.

"The guard will now drop the pellets in."

But as he was about to do so, the General rose and addressed the Court: "Judge, I do not know what you are allowing to take place. But you must know that a man in my position has a dignity to hold. Continue your case. I have done my duty by apprehending the thief and send me the results of your decision to my office. I cannot spend any more of my time here."

But Boris was guarding the only exit.

The General tried to pass him but failed.

Sergei said in a surprisingly loud voice: "The laws of this Court are that no exits or entrances of interested parties can be made during proceedings. Acts appertaining to the Czar's Courts Page 112, Para 14."

"Then I demand special permission!"

Sergei continued, "The activities, which according to General Kornikov himself will take only two minutes, shall be proceeded with." And without awaiting any reaction from the judge, Sergei continued: "Guard, the pellets please."

And Boris turned the key in the great door.

"This door is locked!" raged the General, a dazzling sight in his resplendent uniform.

Boris paused at the glasses. Sergei said, very loudly for him: "We will drop the pellets in. Any man guilty of stealing jewellery must admit before the pellets reach the floor of the glass. If he do so, his punishment shall be light. If he fails to do so and is later found guilty his punishment shall be severe according to the conscience of the Court."

Boris dropped the pellets one by one, beginning with the General's, the ninth glass. 'The Buriats' number,' he thought.

The General had an instinct to knock the glass down again, but that monster of a kulak (which Boris was not) stood too close.

Just as the pellets were reaching the bottom, three grabbed at their glasses. Vassili was one. The other two were the two newcomers.

"Three?" shouted the General, alive again. "Who are these men? I do not know these men!"

Sergei said, but softly so that Boris had to repeat it louder: "Irbit the Lion did not know Ungin, the fox, who stole the big toe. Nor did he know Shono, the wolf, nor Hara Grojung the black bear, nor. . . Might I display a few articles?" Boris took them from Sergei's bed to display them to the Court. "This is a small piece of a coat taken from a brodyagi murdered a hundred miles south of Omsk. Perhaps we could call him Ungin, the fox? Ungin stole the big toe. Here is the lapel of a soldier's jacket and a buckle from his horse slaughtered fifty miles south of Omsk. Should we call him Shono, the wolf? Here are buttons from the livery of one of the eighty servants from the Estate of Marianovka" – There was a gasp. The General had an Estate at Marianovka – "who, shall we say, stole the big toe." One of the eighty servants – in the dock – one of the two newcomers, bowed his head. "This epaulette is from the Third Siberian Regiment" – Kornikov's regiment. The second of the newcomers in the dock bit his lip and grabbed the rail before him – "Who stole the toe."

"And you'll be saying that I am Irbit the Lion next, will you?" shouted the General shaking his frenzied fist at the bed.

Sergei was silent. The judge was silent. The Court was silent. Silent as the grave.

"Well? I've asked a question, you bed-ridden fraud you! I insist on your answer!"

"I ask Gaspazja* Huragina to come forward please."

Two middle-aged Buriats brought an old lady forward from the back of the Court, supporting her by the arms.

*Gaspazja: Mrs

114

She was heavily veiled. But all could see she was not a Buriat.

"Your name, please?"

"Gaspazja Alexandra Stepanova Huragina."

"Your name is Buriat?"

"I am married to the leader of the Western Buriats on the Irtusk, three days south from here."

"Your husband?"

"Was too ill to travel. This, all this, has broken his health."

"You know the prisoner-in-the-dock?"

"He is our only son."

"Why did he come to Omsk?"

"He was bringing the centre piece of my heirloom. He was to sell it through the Bank and my dear husband had promised we could have a real house and end our days in a city."

"You were married before?"

"Engaged."

"Where?"

"In Moscow."

"You had the heirloom then?"

"It has been handed down through generations in our family. It was to go to my husband-to-be."

"Why did you break off your engagement?"

"I fell in love with a wonderful man. I have the remainder of the heirloom with me." She opened a packet on her lap. All were agape at the magnificence of it. "My son, our dear Vassili, travelled with the centre piece only. The wonderment part. The surround was counterfeit. My husband had had a presentiment of attack. So we agreed to keep this true surround in the cask in our yurt, so that we would at least retain something."

"Who were you engaged to?"

"To the Lion."

The General fell to one knee before her and stared up —
stared up —

"Princess Alexandra?"

The old lady raised her veil and bared her face. "Yes, Nikolai Ivanovitch."

Vassili came forward. His mother received her son in her arms.

Kornikov was dead. He had shot himself through the temple.

The Court was silent. Silent as the grave.

48

There is a god in Siberia. And Boris saw it. He was out with his hunters and it was towards the end of March.

"It's there! Look! There! There!"

The little band of ten stopped riveted to the spots they were standing on in their sliding shoes. All necks craned upwards.

The sun caught a tiny white speck in the sky and it gleamed as it passed them over. It was the Arctic bird. No one has even given it any other name. As it will reach further north the Tartars and Tungusi go into a mad joy at the sight of it. No one, whatever the temperature, will remain with his hat on. All, whether with fur, felt or skin on, though it will be only for a moment will grab at their hats, bare themselves as the lone white bird flies over. No one has seen the bird except air-borne.

It is a herald. It signifies that .winter is finishing. It is never late. Soon after it has passed some give it a cheer, but it always passes in silence. It flies to the Arctic Circle

116

and beyond and then returns. No hunter would shoot it. No hunter could live with himself who tried to shoot it.

Boris had heard of it. But heard of it as one of the thousand stories that fireside listeners hear of that noblest landscape on earth: Siberia.

In the far northern latitudes where the sun never rises in the winter, this pure white bird flies so high that the sun catches under its wings so that the first the natives see of the so-awaited sun is the mirrored-reflection under the wings and on that soft down underbelly of this Arctic wonder that no one has a name for. Up there, the sun, and the bird to prove it. Beneath still twilight. Then, by the time it returns, the sun is already shining fully down, and the whole of Siberia knows that the bird was God's harbinger that had brought the sun back to the earth.

49

"Streltzi is roping convicts together in batches, firing in a cannon and betting on how many anyone can kill with one ball," said Boris. "And I'm going to stop him," he ended.

"You're a spoil-sport!" said Sergei.

"That's what I am!" said Boris.

They were sitting with Anton in the Zaitsev Hotel into the evening wait for their meal. Sergei was now mobile enough to live outside the hospital and soon would be completely himself.

"It's true, it's the Talk of the Town," came in Anton. "And he's inviting anyone from anywhere to go to the bloody prison on Sunday and watch the 'finals of the sport'. To join in the betting, too. Hundreds are going."

117

"And you're going to let me help you spoil his fun I hope?" asked Sergei.

"Are you well enough?"

"It would make me ill again to miss it. So. Strelzi made his name as an Ataman by cooking a boy and a girl on a grid, the mother and father being the grid-irons. They couldn't pay their taxes. Ivan the Terrible, Peter the Great, Pugachev, they're all famous like that. Every house in Omsk has a picture on the wall of Napoleon. Yet if he'd come here he'd have made slaves of this lot. So. If it's going against the grain of our countrymen that you want to do, count me in. And we'll spoil a story."

"Count Anton out," said Boris. "He's got to live here. There's Alicia and the kids too. He'll be in on the planning but not on the doing. It'll be two against 200, Sergei."

"Fine. So. But I can tell you something about Cossacks, Anton. So. In case they find out you helped with the planning. So. They wouldn't be interested. Cossacks will be the most ferocious enemies. But they have neither Mongol cunning nor Russian memory. They'll fight like inspired villains till they drop. But if they get up next day still alive, they'll have forgotten their enemies. I like them. They are fierce terrors. But without a grudge. So."

"Anton!" called Boris. "Your health! Then tell us what you know about the prison."

And Boris and Sergei drank the health, then Anton had a 'nip' for fun, then the three heads got close together and Anton began:

"First: the talk of the town. One of Streltzi's lieutenants discovered in an old old shed, an old old cannon, no one can say how old. They heaved it out. There were four of them, Streltzi, Yakov, Streltzi's right hand, and two others who are called the Long and the Short of It, one being tall and the other tiny. They stood

118

round that thing till Streltzi said he'd like to fire it. The Long of It said there was a gun engineer in the prison. So they pulled him out, gave him some decent food and set him to work. Within a day he had fixed it up, prepared some powder of sulphur, saltpetre and charcoal, and Streltzi took the first shot. They got excited like schoolboys and called the prisoners. They tried to hit them one by one and a dozen died. The engineer wept, and no one knows more about him. Soon they ran out to shot. But the 'Remennikov Gun and Ballistics Foundry' was written on one ball and they called in the Manager and he has agreed to try and reproduce them. They announced the contest for Sunday. The four Founder Members of the Sport shall be the sportsmen but the betting is open to all. Zakuski* and kvass will be served and the women are hoping the sun will shine so that they can wear their best. Another drink?"

And they downed more vodkas.

"But do you know the prison?" pursued Boris.

"It's the first camp we're all unloaded into. So it's ten years since I was there. But it's the same I'm sure. Only Streltzi is different."

And he drew them a plan.

50

It happened, by the grace of good fortune, that the Remennikov Gun and Ballistic Foundry employed a large number of Raskalnikovs. The Raskalnikovs were a fanatical religious group, so

*Zakuski: Russian snacks.

uncontrollable in their beliefs that it was with great relief that the Czarist Government heard of their desire to emigrate. They were given every assistance and a large number reached Omsk. Many companies vied for their services. They were well-known for actually working, a most rare virtue, while working-without-fiddling was a bonus no employer dare miss.

Boris and Sergei therefore hurried by droshki next morning to visit the Raskalnikovs' leaders.

Boris and Sergei liked them and they liked Boris and Sergei. The Raskalnikovs were honoured and delighted to be asked to risk their lives to save people, even though the to-be-saved had only a half-hearted wish to live.

And secrecy was nearly the Raskalnikovs' second religion.

Boris and Sergei were asked to return next day to listen to suggestions.

"There's nothing like fanatics for getting things done," said Sergei.

5l

The strangest collection of characters left the eight other Omsk precincts to descend on the northern Cossack village for the Sunday shoot-out. Petty thieves, pettier harlots, hardened gamblers, more-hardened respectable women, men, some arguing, some tight-lipped, about how to place bets in this new field of activity, women, past their prime, hoping to be stirred again in the darker side of their embers where their men had ceased to stir them, the hungry wondering how much kvass and how many zakuski they could down without vomiting, women angry that the Cossacks could not have waited a few weeks till the warm sun would have helped them vie in competitions of finery – alas, it was not Cossack nature to wait, neither do they seem to know what 'weather' is, being impervious to the changes.

The crowds came from their holes or from their twenty stone houses to be united as one for this Carnival Sunday.

The Cossacks had prepared their main exercise yard and its high wall kept out the worst of the swirling winds. Vodka, kumyss and tarasun, had been added to the kvass, and gingerbread and doughnuts added to the zakuski. Prisoners acted as waiters. There seemed no need for guards. . .

It might have been a skittle party on an Oxford lawn, except that this was at below zero between four stark walls under a sheet white sky, and most of the crowd looked that wretched that Oxford would have had to scour the country round to have found a dozen such wretches and that the gambling was fiercer than at a thousand skittle parties. Also the sport was not skittles – or was it? Also, instead of being a lush, sunny Oxford lawn, it must have been the dreariest sports ground since the last Race to the North Pole. But in Omsk's favour it must be said that instead of sedate Oxford, here was liveliness indeed. So, really, the only similarity in the simile to Oxford was – skittles.

Convicts could be roped according to the contestants' wishes: in a circle, in a straight line one behind the other, in a triangle, or, as they fancied. The number was also of their own choice, seven for some, twelve for others. But the number was important because an outright killing was ten points, one unscathed was minus ten, a mere maiming was a straight nil; so the bold aimed for high numbers and the wary chose low.

Announcements were made and bets placed. Each contestant would fire three times. The winner would take half the winnings, and the winner from the betting would take the other half.

Three walls guarded the public. The fourth wall was for the action. A table twenty paces long was reserved for the contestants and Boris and Sergei sat near it.

The convicts were brought in.

Boris said: "They look like cannon fodder. How can it be? There are a hundred of them. Sergei, if you and I were there, wouldn't we do *something*? They look like powder already."

"They are powder already. Hunger and cold have made them so. People only feel as you feel, when their belly is nourished. When the stomach is stoked up, then the mind begins to click."

"I cannot believe that I could die without a gesture of defiance."

"You are a good man, Boris, but there is too much you know nothing of. Yet for now it's Raskalnikovs versus Streltzi. And it's for us to be abnormally alert."

They each pressed each other's knee.

Streltzi led his three lieutenants in amid applause. Streltzi looked the double of the famed Pugachev: round, in every part of him, clothes about him like hoops, almost never standing straight, eyes characterless and beady, strange eyes, tiny, whether he laughed or fumed his eyes never changed, in fact beady was the only adjective for them, for they were of stone yet glossed over, but also abnormally tiny as if a doll maker had stuck in beads two sizes too small, and Boris noticed that later when Streltzi was drunk, his eyes still registered no change. Streltzi's Right Hand, Yakov, who according to reputation had been a heart-stopper in his twenties, was now at forty massive and surly: he also had broadened all round him thereby seemingly

122

diminishing his height and, since they say dogs sometimes pick up the characteristics of their masters, then this, Yakov had done, and he grew more into a Streltzi every year. The remaining members of this notorious quartet lived up to their nick-names, the Long and the Short of It.

The selected convicts were in groups of ten. The contestants sized them up as unemotionally as if selecting bricks for a wall, said how many they wanted in each group, how they wanted them bound, in a circle, in a straight line in depth, faces inwards or outwards, and then placed them at four points.

Streltzi, only, had his group in a circle. Yakov had elected for a triangle with its apex facing the gun. The Long and the Short of It had each chosen a straight line, each prisoner roped behind the other.

A little extra pressure on each other's knee between Boris and Sergei, a sudden silence and Streltzi had fired. The ball took a parabolic curve upwards, flew over the men, over the wall and was never seen again: indeed it left one with the impression that it had taken off for a Round-the-World trip.

Streltzi went mad, yelled for heads to fall, turned his back not to watch Yakov's shot, then stepped up his fuming till half the compound feared they might never see Omsk again. "That's only the first! We have three fires each!" he screamed at the crowd. Yakov cleaned the bore with fat wads of felt, fed in the powder. . . and should have been pleased he had selected a triangular formation as his ball too took to a parabolic flight but sideways instead of upwards and his ball downed Prisoner 62637 on the far row at the back, though it missed all else. And 62637 was dead. But Yakov, although present leader in the stakes went into his own version of Cossack-histrionics and looked likely to threaten the other half of the compound.

"The balls are out of shape and weight," whispered Boris, "though it would need better experts than that pair to spot it."

Amidst the half inferno and half chaos, the Long of It prepared his gun as if he was in an ocean with his ship becalmed.

"The powder's loosely packed for this one – " murmured Boris.

The chaos and inferno persisted but the Long of It fired without warning and the shot died a few feet in front of the barrel, looking silly. Looking pathetic. Looking like a miscarriage.

"Very loosely packed," offered Boris.

This brought a silence upon the crowd. Even more threatening than the hullabaloo.

It became electric.

Streltzi silenced this silence with a master-stroke.

"Twelve posts will be erected in a line. A prisoner roped to each. We Cossacks will gallop past lopping off heads. The rules are the same as before. We will each choose between seven and twelve for our number. Your bets stand but any changes will be honoured. Drinks and zakuski will be served while we prepare the posts and saddle our horses. Tomorrow more heads will fall for the debacle you have witnessed."

A hundred Cossack guards appeared from nowhere, lined the bare wall and shot up to the sky. Soon the tarasun and kvass and zakuski started their healing effects. Everyone began discovering virtue in the new sport that the other never had "And these Cossacks *can* gallop!" agreed all. "*And* wield their sabres!" agreed all. The darker side of the staid women present felt their titillation would have a more aristocratic boost now with this. They might even take their husbands to bed to round the titillation off.

Boris said: "Over there!" And he rushed Sergei over to

a group of six Raskalnikovs who had gloried God and defied the Cossacks to be present. They had white tickets in their peak caps so that the two friends could identify them. Boris said quickly: "Three come with me. We must create every diversion we can think of. Three go with Sergei here. Sergei, as slyly as you can mix the Cossacks' drinks while they are away fetching their saddles. And these good men have brought a mixture to add. Keep the spirits foremost. Hide the wines. If we can, we'll go and have a little influence with the horses too. God's sake men, be careful! We do this for the glory of the good Lord on high! Christ is on our side!"

Twelve posts were driven into the ground at good distances apart. But they were monster square posts more than a chest width on each side. And they swivelled.

After the competitors had selected their numbers required – again some chose seven and others twelve – the convicts were then roped four round each post, so that after each rider had completed his run through, the posts could be swivelled ready for the next.

All agreed that this Cossack version of 'sticking the pig' had much more to it than those dull balls and duller old cannon. And the spirits of all had risen also with the spirits they had imbibed. Indeed the Cossacks had redeemed themselves.

"I really think you should congratulate Ataman Streltzi, my dear," said the deputy Governor's wife to the Deputy Governor.

"I will, my dear. I will."

Side gates at the end of the long clear wall were thrown open so that the riders could ride in and out at the gallop.

All of these four Cossacks were famous for their riding.

125

There was not one of them who could not swipe all heads off at one gallop through. Indeed each had done so elsewhere in the past.

52

Streltzi missed six and claimed two. Then rolled off his horse after missing the last. And passed out sprawled prone.

Yakov hit at the wind but not at the heads. And fell facing number six. "I had greased his saddle," Boris said.

The third rider never appeared. A horse tore through. And out. But there was no one on it.

The fourth got in. Halted. Twisted around and about. No one could decide whether driver or horse was drunk. Then he dashed at the crowd sabre aloft. And the half drunk crowd half sprawled out and no one quite knew what happened because no one had ever been in such a schemozzle before.

In the turbulence that followed the good Raskalnikovs substituted the dud cannon balls for true ones, so that all supplies could now be tested and proved: and Boris and Sergei strolled away.

Poogavitsa and Kukurooza awaited them. Boris took out a hip flask. "Just one?" he asked Sergei.

"Just one," said Sergei.

"Just one," came from a voice behind them. It was the head priest of the Raskalnikovs. The priest took the flask. Put a finger to his lips: "Not a word!" he said. And took a gulp. "How I needed that!" he added. "Not a word!" And he had gone.

126

"Sergei," said Boris, "You accused me of wanting to cheat this town of a good story. What do you think now?"

"I'd say you've replaced one story with another. A happy story for a horror one. Dear friend, homo sapiens prefers a horror story. So. Uh. But to hell with homo sapiens and, as the good Raskalnikovs would agree, you've raised a flag for God today, and that's the best story of all and deserves another drink!"

They emptied the flask between them. Then their horses took them home.

53

A week later the Spring came in in the morning and out in the afternoon, replaced by summer.

By evening Boris and Sergei were riding out of Omsk.

By nightfall they were surrounded at their bivouac by a posse of twelve horsemen who had surrounded their fire in a circle round them.

The two friends instinctively went back to back to face the mob but did not draw guns.

One of the group spoke southern Russian. "We want you to come and meet our leader. Keep your guns and come quietly and all will be well. Draw your guns or don't come and we'll leave you dead on the spot."

"Who is your leader?" asked Boris.

"You'll find out."

"Do we know his name?"

"Are you coming? Or do you prefer to occupy a permanent two paces of ground?"

"That wouldn't do you much good. But then it wouldn't do us much good either. Shall we go Sergei?"

127

"So."

They turned away from the Omsk highway and headed north west towards Kormilovka. They approached the village when the southern Russian said "We are here." And a short way down a path on the right were some six low wooden buildings.

Sergei said: "This is the Cossack camp at Kormilovka. The Cossacks are in control here. They are under the government of Tobolsk but are in the Tiulanisk district. We are forty miles from Omsk and the Trans Siberian Railway passes eighteen miles from here."

They entered and found Streltzi flat out on a make-shift bed in trouble with both legs. Yakov stood beside him.

54

When Zjennia's bull's-hide dress arrived at her home it transformed her.

And when she appeared in the street in it, it transformed Ch——.

In fact Ch—— became Zj——.

The odour at first seduced, and then the heathen-oily-black, black as crushed beetles, sickened the senses.

Ch—— didn't know where it was. But Zj—— knew where she was – on the throne.

She decided to start her new life with confession.

She went to the priest, Alexis. Who from that day on doubled his poetry output, the libido having twice the force of the spiritual. The penis the pen is.

"Priest Alexis," she began. "This confession in a way

128

concerns the morning after my wedding and my pride at displaying the blood on my nuptials' sheet."

"Ah!" said the priest. The whole town had tittle-tattled about that, and a goodly portion of it felt they had experienced proof of its deception.

"I am a puritan," she continued. "I lived for the day when I should give myself to my man unsoiled, unspoiled."

'This is a strange talk, my cherished one,' thought the priest.

"Although many of the men, very many of the men, whose company I enjoyed before my wedding night, had caressed and caroused with me, none broke me. Almost all were somewhat inebriated when they made their assault: Mother had taught me the art of cupping my legs so that the illusion of entering my body was granted without my virginity becoming surrendered. I have deceived *so very many men* Priest Alexis. I have come to ask forgiveness."

Alexis' first thought was neither a priestly nor a godly one: had she deceived him too: in their week of glory?

"I want to be absolved from my sin. Deceiving so many. I was indeed virgin on my nuptials' night."

He looked at her: was overcome: words would have choked him. So he signed that he absolved her. And he immediately began on more unpriestly, ungodly thoughts: 'How can I get her to come again? What other confession does she stand in need of?'

129

55

Leaving the church precincts Zjennia met the butcher's boy entering to make his confessions.

She rested her hand on the youth's shoulder and said: "The priest is busy now. He is busy writing. Come back with me Alochik and you can make your confessions to me."

And, confused, he left with her. And for the rest of his life he was to declare he had never been the same since that day.

Zjennia took him later home. Then stayed on with the butcher himself.

Who also declared he had never been the same again since his experiences that day.

Thus it was with both Ch—— and Zj——.

They have never been the same since the arrival of that bull's-hide.

56

Streltzi now said his name was Plakhanov. Yakov said his name was Krakinov.

Streltzi, from his sick bed, asked the newcomers: "Will you have tea or kumyss?"

"Russian tea?"

"The best. Don style."

"Then tea for me," said Boris. "And for you, Sergei?"

"So."

"You had an accident to your leg, Sergei I think your name is? And were in the Omsk hospital?"

"That's right."

"I have had an accident to both my legs. I fell from my horse a week ago. This is my lieutenant, Captain Krakinov. He fell too. We were both fouled. His fall was not serious and he has recovered. Your doctor must come to me."

Streltzi, now Plakhanov, added that he would hold them hostage against the visit of the doctor.

"I must have paper," said Sergei.

"Don't tell him I want him. Tell him you want him."

Sergei chanced his luck and put in many a hint.

"What is this?" asked Streltzi, staring at the paper.

"The doctor and I are from a small community group near Yaroslav. It's our patois. He speaks and understands Russian, but this way he knows for sure the letter comes from me."

Streltzi darkened his brows but let it pass.

A messenger came and set off.

The two friends were given a room and were guarded. But they were fed well and were unmolested.

Dr. Yusopoff chanced his luck and came. But he didn't chance his language and spoke with Sergei in their patois.

Plakhanov (Streltzi) had broken both legs just below the knee, and would need many months before he could walk again. "Yet however had he been withstanding the pain for the week?"

"I want you to come back in some days," asked Sergei, "in case we have not got away. You know how it is in these situations: if an outsider knows, a man is half-clear. And you warn your friends too in Omsk that you are coming."

131

When the doctor had left, Plakhanov sent for Boris and Sergei.

The two button-eyes looked at them — it wasn't a stare. Those eyes seemed incapable of anything but just looking.

"What?"

"You are my prisoners."

After a pause he added "I have a proposition." He paused again. "One of you has to become a Cossack for a summer. Unless you prefer a coffin."

He paused again.

"Every year," he continued, "we set out from here or near here collecting taxes. It takes us most of the summer. Krakinov and I take two men with us. I can't go this year. One of you will have to."

"Why not your other men?"

"What other men? There's only Krakinov and myself."

"Then why one of us?"

"You are not chaff. I know your type. Even though you're Russian. Or Yaroslavski as you pretend. There's a lot of money in this. A hell of a lot. I need one of you. I'm damned if I'm going to explain."

"And if we don't go?"

"You're dead!" Streltzi was seized in a rage. "I'm offering you your life and a fortune. What do you want? A fortune, or two lengths of soil in the nearest field?" He fumed.

"How do we get the fortune?"

"Half the damn profits! Could you dream of more? I think you want your graves."

"How is this half?"

"One of you goes and you go with Krakinov. You pick up a fortune. You and Krakinov a fortune each. Krakinov will tell you all the ropes, the prices: he will fix the taxes, his word will be final but you are his equal

132

for making a fortune because you go as my deputy. When you return you lay all your profits before me. We each take half and you are on your way. You never had a fairer deal in your life. Take it. Or I'll take your life and am angry enough to do so now."

Boris rose: "Ataman Plakhanov, I need a word with my friend alone."

Plakhanov looked slyly at him. From near the bottom of his lips he grunted: "Put your guns on the table and go back to your room and come back in five minutes."

Sergei and Boris left.

"Will he kill us if we don't do it?" asked Boris.

"So."

"But why can't he use his own men?"

"Either because he knows they are unreliable. Or because few of them know the rules of the game and this way none of the others get ideas of aggrandisement."

"Does he suspect us of anything in Omsk?"

"Uh. I don't know. Perhaps yes. Perhaps no. So."

"Sergei, I am sorry, I have to tell you one thing."

"What?"

"I will explode if I do not get into action. If we draw lots for who goes and you win I just cannot guarantee my controlling myself."

"I can stay. The doctor can bring me books and friends. Only hurry back the best you can. I have a problem however. Uh. Huh. So."

"And that?"

"I had planned to reach Chita this summer. Leave that to me. I'll fathom something. I'll get the doctor to visit Streltzi here every Sunday. And I'll send for a chess friend. I'll like that. Try if you can to manoeuvre your return for a Saturday. I'm getting ideas. Uh. Huh. So."

"Do you trust the Cossacks?"

"As much as anyone. Which is not much. It's only our lives we want out of this. I'll think about our lives. You think about our fortune. You are being taken in at the top level. You'll learn about the Czar's methods of peaceful penetration."

They returned to Streltzi.

"Ataman Plakhanov," said Boris. "Are we to take it that you are keeping one of us against the other? That if one of us does not return with the fortune, the other's life is at stake? And if the one who stays, escapes, the first one's life is at stake?"

Plakhanov did not answer, but glared.

"Ataman Plakhanov," Boris continued. "One thing is not clear. Why cannot Krakinov do this alone? Why, as it were, do you need two tax collectors?"

"We stretch ourselves to the limit. And when we have reached last year's outposts the two of you will take one companion each and add one town, or two villages to our territory. It is our rule, then you meet up again and return. At the end of last year's territory you'll act like a fork with two prongs. And no more bloody explaining."

"It is I who will go," said Boris. "You threaten me. But now I threaten you. If one hair of my friend's head is harmed in my absence a whirlwind will arise which will sweep you to instant death. To hell with your threats to me! I am going with Krakinov," and he slapped Yakov on his shoulders, "and we are going as friends. Sergei and I accept your bargain. But not your threats. Yet you better keep your part of the bargain else you'll find my threats as a sabre against your paper-knife. When do we start?"

Plakhanov did not answer.

57

It was on the fourth day out that the small party of four turned off a small path into a village.

Tax collecting was about to begin. They had journeyed north east along small roads and Boris never found out the name of that first stop.

The village had big cabin houses in pairs. Entrances from the yards at the side and all houses raised to a man's height with storage space underneath for logs, ploughs, and for anything that couldn't go into the simple home. There was a split in the middle of the village and Boris learnt there were two communities, Khirghis families at one end and Russian families at the other.

The children started the stir as they rode in and it was obvious that respect was already theirs. They stopped at perhaps the only imposing building, an eight-roomed log cabin, and they got a bowing and scraping reception.

They tethered their horses, then Krakinov, who had now become Yakov again, swaggered in with the three others. Two sumptuous couches were inside. Yakov took one and motioned to Boris to take the other. Already someone was at Yakov's feet struggling to get his boots off. Boris bent to untie his but Yakov said: "Let them do it!"

So for the first time ever Boris had his boots removed for him. And found it pleasant.

Small stools, or tables, were at their sides. Tea, vodka and gingerbread were brought.

The room was all attention, though the other two Cossacks had been led to other quarters.

Yakov was not as tall as he had seemed in Omsk. He also had two chins and seemed in the process of gaining a third. He looked like a thick oak tree. He never smiled. He was curt to Boris but never rude. He could shout at his lieutenants however and was like a possessed wild animal when he did so.

"What do you want?" he coldly asked Boris. "You don't pay for anything here or anywhere on this trip. We are given everything. New horses, a woman, any drink, any food. That's Russian tea you have. Khirghis if you prefer it."

"Russian tea always," said Boris. "So this is a divided village?"

"Bloody crazy. I don't know what the f—king authorities are up to. Half are Khirgiz families, and half are Russian and now ten more Russian families just arrived. F—k my dear old mother, it's shit crazy. We'll go through two villages together, you and I: then, after you have the idea, we'll do half a village each. That's the only way to get through things. You'll be given your own books – you can bloody well write I hope?"

"Yes."

"If not, they'd find you some crook to do it for you. You make what you can. I make what I can. And we keep it separate."

"Except that I share with Plakhanov?"

"Plakhanov? Oh, Streltzi. Yes you share with Streltzi. You can send your goods home or have them sold in the market. You send to Kormilovka or you carry them with you. That's your own bloody choice. We send all ours to Tobolsk and they are held there."

"How do we send?"

"By f—king post. Post is free to us. And we only handle villages on Post Roads. Tell these buggers what you want to eat, and what you want to drink now. I always get the bloody tax garbage out of the way as quick as I can then stay on a couple of days before moving."

136

There seemed about ten fawns kowtowing about and Boris began taking to it. The fawns even left the room moving backwards, faces to their Cossack masters all the way.

A man entered, bowed obsequiously, but was the chief elder and was of obvious substance.

He sat on a stool opposite them.

"Get rid of this rabble," said Yakov. And the worms did their doubling-back act and left through a centre door as if sucked backwards by a suction pump.

"Ten more bloody Russians?" asked Yakov.

"Ten! It's because we've got that church I suppose."

"Better make the Khirghis go Christian if this goes on. Has the shaman gone?"

"Not yet. He will go. You see he was born here and asked to die here."

"He bloody well will die here if he hasn't left by morning. Get rid of the sinister prick. You've got till early morning to do it. Else we'll stick a pole up his ass and out at his neck and show the whole bloody commune what heathens can expect. Tell the priest I want to see him in the morning. Here are the purchase prices till next winter. Let Boris here see them, after you've seen them."

And Boris in his turn read: "One woman = four sheep. One cow = eight sheep. One horse = thirty two sheep. One gun = ninety six sheep."

Trying to be frivolous Boris asked: "Where are the women coming from?"

Yakov glared: "The Czarist Government send 20,000 prostitutes a year out here. And bloody good women they are too. If the Muscovites had any sense they'd keep the prostitutes back home and send their married trash out. But the 20,000 are for the Russians. For the Khirghiz: any Khirghis will sell you any woman for one sheep, let alone four."

"And are they good too?"

"No fun," and Yakov sounded as if he meant it. "Might as well marry the sheep and save the exchange. I want to see the heads of these ten new families."

"I asked them to come. I have them outside," said Babar.

"Then cheer up you miserable sod!" blurted Yakov. "We are not putting you on the menu for tonight."

"Yes." And Babar feigned the saddest of smiles and fetched the Russians.

"And come back with them!" shouted Yakov. "We might fancy you for the meal yet!"

Ten Russians, half young, half middle-aged, filed in. Everyone's head bowed a little.

"Hallo you sods! This is my partner in misery, Boris. We will tell you your rights, you are to tell me whether this miserable cheat, Babar, has given them to you. Then we'll tell you what's going to happen. You are emigrants? No convicts? Were you told when you signed on you were to be sent to a half Khirghiz commune?"

"No."

"None of you?"

"No."

"So much for the shit you've left behind you. Well, make the most of here and get your rights. We come here twice a year and you complain to us. Take no powers yourself. We'll see you right. Are you all Greek Orthodox Church?"

They were. "Then that simplifies that. No Old Believers? No Raskalnikovs? No shamanists? Listen, I'm going to read your rights. Tell me if you've got them. Then I'll tell you the rest. One house each, if not, one shelter till they or you have built the house. Six acres of field and two acres of wood each in the commune woodland. One horse, one cow, two sheep, one plough,

138

one harrow, one cart, one sickle, those axes that you need: nine puds of seed-corn, nine puds of rye, one of barley, one of oats, one of hemp seed. You are to pay no taxes for three years. After three years you pay ten per cent of your year's takings to the fantastic generous bastard-riddled Czarist Government who nobly offer you all their protection and the dubious right of being its citizens; ten per cent to us lot who do all the real protecting, all the true trading, all the buying and selling for you and you are never to trade with anyone else under any excuse. We'll settle your differences, worry about the Khirghis if they worry you, worry about this weedy fraud Babar — don't let him cheat you brothers, take your rights and bloody good luck to you and have I forgotten anything?"

"Er. . ." said someone.

"Don't er!" shouted Yakov. "Shout out or get your guts washed out! Don't er, man, I'm here to listen!"

Yakov had passed the lists to Boris to read.

"You said nothing about women and children?"

"What about them?"

"How much for each?"

"Good for you! What's your name?"

"Fedor Markovitch."

"A Jew?"

"Yes."

"But you said you'd go to the church?"

"I will. I prefer that to no building of worship. I go in my own hours."

"We don't mind Jews. We like them. Give me that list Boris. You're right. Grants from the Peasant Bank for women and children. Trust a Jew to point that out. Don't take that hard. You are right to ask. One silver kopeck per day, per woman, per child. Have you had it?"

"Not for our children."

"Any of you had it for children?"

None had.

"Babar, you bloody scoundrel you. You will be on the bloody menu tomorrow night the latest. You pay these men double what you owe them out of your own pocket, and pay them by tomorrow morning, else we'll put you on little skewers and have a schaslik party! Look here men, watch this dog. Get your rights. But don't ask for what you have no right to in case you also become the schaslik. Any more questions? You came here of your own free will. The Czarist Government made you promises. We are here to see those promises are kept and we'll squeeze them back there, or here with this miserable toad Babar, to see that we get every ounce of promise made. Don't overstretch yourself though. That puts us against you. We're here for three days. Don't waste our time with trifles, but a serious question and we are here because we are on your side. Babar is on your side too, only you have to kick him up his ass to remind him."

And he had finished so they filed out.

"Markovitch?" Yakov called. "Do you know why you are here? You asked for this commune?"

"No."

"Then I'll tell you why you're here. Where are you from? Kazan? Moscow?"

"Kiev."

"Then you're here because those bastards back in Kiev are a bloody incompetent lot. You should be with a Jewish commune. The next man out will be Ataman Streltzi. I'll tell him. If you want to go to your own kind we'll see that you do so. Just tell us. And if anyone calls you a Jew, tell the priest. I'll see that he handles it. His bloody Christ was a Jew. Good luck."

And he offered Markovitch his hand.

Alone, Boris said: "You were good to the Jew."

Yakov shrugged his shoulders. "Good people," he

140

said. "Work well. Bloody good women in bed. You should try one."

58

The shaman was dead. Murdered in the night. Babar brought the news to Yakov. Yakov seemed uninterested. "He said he wanted to die here. Send the priest in."

Boris asked: "What's wrong with a shaman?"

Yakov knit his eye-brows fiercely and glared harshly at Boris.

"Any man is perfectly free to worship in any religion he likes – any organised religion."

"Why is organised religion all right?"

Yakov fumed: "It's organised, isn't it? Is there anything else you want to know? If it is organised we control it!"

"You can't control a shaman?"

"Shamans are either upstart heroes or local gods. Heroes and gods should stay where they belong. Up there!" And he pointed to heaven. "If they're up there they're easy to handle."

"Doesn't the Metropolitan of Moscow control the Church?"

Yakov spat: "Ppppp! Ah, here's our good man himself."

And a mild priest walked in.

"Ah, I have an especially good day for you," began Yakov. "You're going to conduct a funeral for a shaman."

"For Kensha Kara?"

"How did you know?"

The priest was shocked beyond measure and refused hotly. "Such a witch of a man."

"It gives you a unique chance to get his followers inside your precincts. I advise you to do as we suggest. The next church from here is in an Ostiak area. And there they have the principle that a priest should be killed before they themselves die so as to be at heaven's gates to receive them when they die themselves, but after you've had time to put in a word for them before their arrival. Don't worry. They respect you and always put wine and victuals in your coffin to see you on your way. But don't bury Kensha Kara here. There must be no marking of his grave. I think we could say it was his last wish to be buried in the River Ob where he'll get washed out to the Arctic Ocean? We have much to do now, your reverence, the Khirghiz have come to pay their tributes. Good-bye."

59

The Khirghiz came in one by one. Babar had a record of each man's profits for the year.

Babar said what the year had proved best for, and from that Yakov fixed the barter. Money was never taken though the Czar's percentage was always paid over in roubles.

Yakov fixed the barter in hides and sheepskins or equivalents. An equivalent which was forever on the list was sable: one sable would clear any man for a year: that is to say, one sable for the Czar and one for the Cossacks. But sables were almost non existent this far

142

south and were not to be expected. Yakov called Boris over and they went through the first man's hides together. Both men were impressed though neither said so to the farmer. Yakov accepted nine. The man held two more in reserve. One was taken. Five for the Czar of all the Russias: five for the protectors and governors, the Cossacks.

"I wish they were all so simple," said Yakov.

It seemed clear that Yakov was keeping all those profits from this village for himself with no percentage for Boris. Perhaps he would later give Streltzi a percentage. Boris said nothing.

Things went well until one came in who wanted his part to be accepted in grain but begged and pleaded that he could not meet the demands. He had had disaster after disaster.

"Then," said Yakov. "You will find it easier to meet your debts for the future if you have no wife or children to supply for. Bring your wife and two children here and we will sell them in the next market."

The wretch plunged to the ground, kissed Yakov's boots, begged Babar to explain, torrented out his miserable disaster after disaster, whimpered, screamed. . .

"If you say one more word," raged Yakov as if a scorpion had just built a nest in his entrails, "I'll take your family whatever you do. We are here for three days, if you pay up your taxes before then you can take your miserable tribe back. Out!! One more word and. . ." The man had gone. Abject. Boris had rarely seen a wretch so broken.

They stopped for refreshment. Boris saw that Yakov was instantly calm and he realised that the flare of heat like a volcano at its height had been an act, a game. . .

"I know these people," was a phrase Yakov used once. Boris did not forget it.

143

In this case the man paid the next day and amid incredible emotion the wife, the boy and the girl were returned to him.

Boris didn't know these people. What would he do when it came to his demanding his pound of flesh? That he would have to face those who would put on convincing displays of inability to pay, and that he would also meet up with the genuine hard-hit suppliants, were both certain: and that he would be unable to sort out one from the other was equally certain. Yakov had no such problem: it was 'pay up or else. . .'

A man came in and laid out two pelts. Sables! And a story about his wife having had them for years and now, as they were unable to meet the tax, being willing to let them go.

Yakov and Boris looked them over. Boris knew they weren't sable, and whatever they were they had been doctored. Each man held one in his hand. Yakov turned in towards Boris and looked him in the eye. Boris said nothing, but certainly could not bring himself to declare them genuine.

"Put your arm on the table," said Yakov quietly to the man. The man did so.

Yakov went to his couch and came back with a sabre.

"Tell your wife, if she prefers you with no hands to send us in two more sables next year."

And Yakov raised the sabre. And a hand jumped away from a wrist and made a little arc then fell on the ground looking lost.

60

The priest came and invited Yakov to the church. "The church is near. And the road is slippery from the melting snows, so we cannot come."

Babar came and invited Yakov to the inn.

"The inn is far. And the road is slippery from the melting snows. But if we tread carefully we should reach there.

And the four left with Babar for the inn.

The atmosphere which had been apprehensive, tensed and with people half hiding from sight, was now easy-going and lazy.

Taxing was done, tributes were over for a year, only one hand had been sacrificed and that already forgotten, the bees were buzzing, flowers were busy making carpets in the alley-ways, and except for the general wretchedness that was ever pervasive, life returned to its one true occupation: the passing of time.

Yakov, who Boris had decided must be considered a monster, was relaxed himself and greeted by all around. Even obsequity had gone. Yakov had been sucked inside the tranquillity and even his village hetman, Babar, and he now walked to the inn as brothers. And with never a rude word.

It was usual to have some Cossack sports, mostly riding prowess and spearing hoops, or rabbits, at the gallop, but Yakov had said they would not have them this year. Was he still pondering over his fall in Omsk?

The church rang a bell and although most citizens trailed past it and preferred the call of the inn, the bell

145

was the pride not only of the church but of Russian and Khirghiz citizens alike. With the installing of that bell, a gift from the Czar at the suggestion of Streltzi, the village basked in glory.

Half the inn were busy gambling. A quarter played chess. And the rest scandalized. Ivan, eighty-three, had just been refused marriage by Maria aged sixty: so he felt he should celebrate. It would have been his fifth bride, and he wanted to rejoice that he was not going to get encumbered for a fifth time.

Yakov gambled. He contested fiercely, took defeat glumly, but never showed anger.

Of the two other Cossacks, Petr, 'The Short of It', had been one of the four at the Omsk fiasco. He constantly eyed Boris wondering where he had seen him before. The other, Djugashvili, was dreamy, looked capable of slyness and was constantly lazily smiling. He took up a balalaika and the whole inn got caught in his songs, one Cossack melody after another. Petr then challenged the village champion to a wrestling match, Mongolian style, and won. The two men sparred for an opening for ten minutes, each like a bent pin, the body from the waist up being parallel to the floor, then, in a dart, Petr was in and the match was settled in seconds.

Markovitch came to Yakov and said he wanted to grow tobacco. Yakov, temporarily not gambling, listened.

"I grew tobacco in the Ukraine. There is fine soil for it by Lake Artugan five miles from here. I have spoken to the new families. Six want to join in. But it seems the whole village, both communities, are most anxious. Especially as it's tobacco I want to grow."

"And you need money to start it off?"

"That's the problem."

"That's no problem. If you need money you get it from us. We haven't got it. But the Banks have. And we get it

146

for you. You have to purchase the land to begin with. Three roubles per desiatin. Come with us and with Babar here, to Tatarskoye in two days, work out a beginning estimate for the whole commune, and we will raise you a loan for your needs." The land actually belonged to nobody. The Czar might say it was his. Meanwhile Yakov decided it was his.

"You should be in Kainsk," said Yakov. "The Government are trying to make a Jewish colony there, but they are exploiting them. They always exploit Jews. They'll send you there if you leave here. But if you stay here the Ataman, Streltzi, favours Jews and we'll see you right."

After Yakov had accepted another drink from the innkeeper, he continued with Markovitch: "Be wary of making common cause with the others here, Markovitch. Their enthusiasm for your exploits will be in this room over kumyss and vodka. Not out there in the fields. I suggest we sell land to them all in their enthusiasm. Then you work your own plot. If they want the tobacco enough they'll then work their land. If not, they'll want to buy off you, which they can do through us."

"They've shown enthusiasm. And they all smoke."

"Encourage them, Markovitch. We will be behind you. But work your own plot only. If you put a circle 5000 miles around this village you are in now you'd be putting a circle around laziness where it is not a word but the chief occupation. But they all love tobacco. You are on to a great experiment. Just don't be sucked in by their talk. Be an example and we'll all watch. Be ready to leave in two days for the Bank loan. Babar will give you a horse. Why don't you want to go to Kainsk?"

"I want to live where I can forget I am a Jew."

The Jew left. Feeling proud.

Yakov said to Boris "I've just sold some land that I

never knew existed, and the Ataman and I should soon have free tobacco for life," Yakov glowed contented as a cobra full of warm milk.

Boris picked up Djugashvili's balalaika, strummed a few bars, then sang Samara's masterpiece: Stenka Razin.

Yakov gaped with wonderment.

He asked for a dance. Boris handed the balalaika to Djugashvili. He played a Lesginka.

Yakov danced. Grotesque. Like a frog making full use of his legs. But the rhythm and the ebullience in that fat form!

Then Boris asked for the balalaika again. And sang the Song of the Volga.

A grey grim village in the middle of an empty Siberian vastness became a light and rose up burnishing like a star, raised there aloft for this short spell by four most dubious tax collectors.

61

When the party of six prepared to leave, Poogavitsa was nowhere to be found.

"Where's my horse?" Boris shouted.

Yakov said: "We all get new horses at every stop. The best. That's a fine black mare you have."

Boris tore off the saddle and flung his bags to the ground.

"Poogavitsa goes with me or I'll see you in hell!"

"Poogavitsa! What a name! And never a horse!" Yakov began working himself up like Satan with a tooth-ache. "We Cossacks are ashamed and refuse to ride with it!!"

148

Boris saw Poogavitsa grazing in a field. He slowly went to it. He slowly marched back with it. He saddled it up, added the stirrups and his bags and mounted.

Yakov never spoke to Boris all day.

Markovitch rode with Boris. "There was to be a third pogrom in my life-time when I decided to apply for emigration. All I want is to forget that I am a Jew. I want to be Fedor Markovitch and not to think, or to be made to think, of anything else. Can I believe it about your Ataman?"

"Give it a try. I will arrange with Yakov that you must never be referred to as a Jew. But if you want to leave, use that as your only excuse, that you need the company of your own brethren. And go to Kainsk."

Two days ride and they were at Tatarskoye. Yakov immediately despatched a messenger for the managers of the Mariupolski, Padin, Soshovsky, Popel and Weiss factories to come to meet him.

The party did not ask for an appointment with the State Bank manager. They brushed in and were told he was busy. They brushed on into his office, scattered three clients, and Yakov sat, feet on the manager's desk and horse-whip beside it. He motioned to Boris to pull up a chair. He was very civil to Boris.

"You know our manager, Babar," he said across the desk to the disturbed official. "This is his assistant, Markovitch, in a joint venture to grow tobacco. They need a loan to put the crop on its feet." And he handled his whip.

"I will be glad to look into it. I hope that we can arrange it. I will speak to my superiors in Omsk and when I have all the details I will be happy to give you our answer."

Yakov raised his whip a short height and let it crack down harshly.

"You will be told by Babar and Markovitch how much

149

they need. You will grant the loan at three per cent interest. You can then tell who the bloody hell you like and tell them that it has been sanctioned jointly by Ataman Streltzi and Prince Galitzin, your Managing Director of your Head Office at Tobolsk. I am busy." He raised his whip again to a short height and cracked it down. "Come Boris we cannot waste time here."

Back at the hotel where they were staying one night at Tatarskoye the managers of the butter factories known as Mariupolski, Padin, Soshovsky, Popel and Weiss awaited the Cossacks.

Yakov ordered a meal for all, but did not hold back his news and addressed them together.

"You probably know that the five of you produce the best butter for a thousand miles around."

They liked that and purred agreement.

"What you don't know is that in future it's Danish butter. Danish butter, with all the transport from Denmark, with import duties, and with its reputation as the best butter on earth, will be cheap at one and a third times your price. We will split the difference with you and I have labels with me. You can have them copied: Alexandrov's Printing Works on Peter the First Square is as good a place as any to copy them. There you are, look: 'Real Danish butter: imported by fast ship and rail'. Stick the labels on.

"Yes Popel?"

"I was just thinking. My family's name: our great grandfather started the enterprise. A fine tradition and reputation."

"So," said Yakov, "Popel prefers his grandfather's, or was it your great-grandfather's? name to one sixth extra profit. But that still leaves four of you, and perhaps if markets move the way we expect in St. Petersburg and Moscow, you might soon be picking up some of Popel's trade as well. . ."

Popel was splattering. He was really only asking for time to consider it and to put it to his board.

"You all use the Trans-Siberian Railway now, but we are enquiring about using the steamers on the Irtush and Volga. Yet for the moment, here are sample labels. Petr and Djugashvili go and see if our meal will be ready before tomorrow. Help yourself to drink gentlemen. Soshovsky you are from the Volga. Did you know the Volga has lost its best bass singer?"

"How is that?"

"He is with us here. Boris has a voice as deep as Chaliapin's. Toady up to him and he might give you a song before we all part. Unless we are dead from starvation first."

62

There were more barbarities at the next settlement, Pokrovsk.

A father was sick and could not visit the Cossacks so sent his eighteen-year-old son to pay the taxes. Over the years of his youth the son had built up an abject terror of the Cossacks and after a few words with Yakov he suddenly bolted. Yakov had him caught, then led to the centre of the main highway and with immense nails a hand's length long the youth was pinned through the centre of each foot to the earth-road: no one was allowed to feed him or to sympathise with him and he was to remain thus riveted till the Cossacks left days afterwards. The screams went on deep into each night.

Then Yakov ordered ten women to be sent to the house and Boris, Petr and Djugashvili were told that he,

Yakov, had no intention of travelling with monks any more, they should select a wench or as many as they wished and spend the night doing what men were put on earth to do.

"Are the women married or virgin?" asked Boris.

"They are ports in a storm, my friend."

Boris had second selection, after Yakov, and his choice was neither beautiful nor ugly, neither young nor old and, as far as he could at first judge, neither willing nor unwilling.

But Boris had a personal problem which he found he could not overcome. His was the choice of nine girls, and that was not choice enough. Though he might be offered the country's finest flower, unless he had personally selected her from out of the wide world he found that did not fit his nature. When in his teens a friend had said "Boris you must meet Olga, she's a black-haired dream," he found that because it was another's estimation and not his own, that already blocked a portion of his lust. The choice must always be wholly his and his alone then – to the conquest.

So here was Luba, born in Pokrovsk, married in Pokrovsk, behaving as if neither willing nor unwilling, and Boris, the most appallingly mixed up male sexually for the whole district round. Ivan Rakovitch, Boris's best friend in Samara, would have advised "Boris, put a sack over your head, and imagine Luba is Zjennia and get on with doing what is expected of you."

Luba came and sat close to Boris. "I am sorry," she said, "I have my period. What are we to do?"

Boris put his two great hands on to her two slender arms, and burst out laughing: "Then we'll have the two greatest glasses of Russian tea ever made!"

And she fell in love with Boris on the spot!

And both, down the years, remembered each other and that evening with warmth.

63

       But Luba had not been good for Boris. Her closeness had unhinged him sexually even more. Zjennia now not only occupied all his night-dreams, she took over his day-dreams as well.

At the next village Boris would be given half the taxing to do and he had to decide on his approach. With Zjennia constantly infringing on his thinking he could only think of the issue by dragging her into it.

'Get all you can for me!' she blurted out a command from nowhere. 'And I want a sable!'

'This is a Cossack matter. Not a Zjennia matter!'

'Then make me a Cossack. Twenty times more demanding than Streltzi, who you are getting half the loot for.'

'Listen! Streltzi and Yakov say to themselves: "What is best for the Cossacks?" Then, foul or fair, they go about getting it. And no other law or moral stands in their way.'

'No they don't,' came Zjennia's marshmallow voice, 'Streltzi and Yakov care no more for the Cossacks than for the Czar or for the communes. They ask themselves what's best for Streltzi and Yakov? And you are acting for Streltzi. And half goes to you. Which is to me. So get every sable and bear skin you see!'

And Zjennia was right, but, forgetting Zjennia – as if he could – and substitute Sergei – why shouldn't Boris squeeze every rouble out of all this he could? He had been temporarily plunged into a wrong world: the fact was that there should be no taxation at all. Streltzi and

Yakov had no rights, the Cossacks had no rights, the Czar had no rights. The St. Petersburg Government had none. But could he, Boris, in this short spell, put all that right? For Streltzi, for Sergei and for himself he should take all he could. And that should be his only guiding thought. Except that he must cut out barbarities.

'Zjennia, it seems I agree with you.'

'Mmmmm.' Oh that marshmallow voice.

64

They reached the river Kuzhurla. On the opposite bank was the next settlement they were visiting.

A smallish boat pulling a raft made the transport for the crossing.

As the ropes were untied for leaving, Boris suddenly saw that the horses had not been taken.

He jumped up and shouted: "Stop! The horses!"

But the boat had left.

"We all get new horses on the other side," said Yakov calmly.

"I bloody well don't! Turn this boat back!"

"It's too late. We are going with the tide."

Boris rose to his threatening height, strode across the boat, picked up Yakov like a leaf, held him over the edge. . .

"Look behind you," said Petr.

"Why? What?"

"Just look."

Still holding on to his strangely quiet arms-full, he turned his head. Poogavitsa had walked to the water and was testing it.

He backed from the water. Walked a few paces down the bank, and then into the water and he tested again.

Again he tracked back.

And again.

Boris turned with his unbelievably docile bundle, a bundle that had become as inactive as a stalled hearse in a snowstorm, and held him once more over the water. He was oblivious of the weight he was holding.

Poogavitsa went a fourth time into the water. Up to the knee once more. This time he continued into it. Just as the depth reached his underbelly, he threw himself on to his side and like a gross blown-up pig's bladder, he floated. And he floated down stream. Soon he was some way out into the river, floating like a corpse. He was keeping pace with the boat itself.

Boris flung his load back to its seat.

"Ha! What do you think of that? Christ, what a horse! Yakov, you f—king traitor, you have been saved by a button! Ha!" He slapped Petr on the back. "Ha!" He slapped Djugashvili on the back. "Ha!" He glared at Yakov. And then he jigged on the spot.

"Come on! Come on!" He called over the railing to Poogavitsa. "Come on! Come on! He's coming!" he called to everyone.

Boris glowed. What pride he felt! Zjennia, what do you think of that?

The boat reached its landing-stage. And twenty paces down Poogavitsa flipped himself upright and walked calmly up to the bridle-path.

Boris was already running down the path to greet him.

As Boris was returning that evening Yakov came and sat quietly on the edge of his bed. "I cannot swim," he said. Then he got up and went away.

65

It was at the point where the fork became two prongs. Petr was to go with Boris. Djugashvili with Yakov. Boris would have preferred it otherwise, but said nothing. Petr was dour and still left Boris with the impression that he recognised him from Omsk.

They were received rapturously at their first destination and were entertained with abundant hospitality. They were accepted as travellers passing through and it was not realised until they met the Elder that they had come to discuss trade and taxes.

Every house had a skin or bits of skin outside it on a pole and this was a mark of reverence to gods that their shaman was in touch with.

It was a happy commune and the most prosperous Boris had seen since leaving Kormilovka.

66

Boris left alone to visit Budar, the shaman. He had never met a shaman before but had heard of them as sinister figures with the powers of witchcraft and a dragging, backward influence on all around them.

Budor was squat on the floor, legs bent under each

other and pots before him which gave out incense mostly aromatic and pleasing. Tea was immediately brought and Boris sat opposite against two cushions.

"I saw that you were coming. I saw it in a trance. You should know that I know you represent the Cossacks, though no one else in the commune realises it.

"You will come here and charm us with irresistible trading offers. You have brought gifts for the Elders and all is sweet and the paths are bedecked with flowers. Your last gesture before departing is to put sentry-boxes at both ends of our commune and you will record the goings and comings of all visitors, and even our Elders. But you will claim it as signifying nothing. Next year your sentry-boxes become huts and houses follow. Four of your kind settle here and take turns for duty at our borders. They discourage outside trade and show us the wisdom of keeping our wares solely for you. You increase your prices if that helps, or decrease them if it seems feasible without disturbing the waters.

"A year or two later you will question my authority and offer us a priest or a mullah whichever we prefer. The point of a priest or a mullah is that it can bring wealth to us, your Christ comes with a church, Allah brings a mosque. Look around and see what they give a shaman. You offer us your influence to help us become citizens of the Czar and the pride of a link with Moscow and St. Petersburg is something that makes us feel important. You like to point out that I am heathen, I believe in no true God, and my trances and medicines are fraudulent.

"I have given my life for this community. It is prosperous because of my ability to leave my body, to see fair or foul weather before it reaches here, to tune in on the migration of birds and deer, so that always my brothers can plant the right crops and prepare to hunt the right flesh and skin. Because I know each family

157

intimately, I can in a trance go to the sources of their maladies and by inner feelings and with their faith in me I keep the commune healthy.

"The Christian and the Mohamedan Gods are inventions kept conveniently distant, and such religions can be manipulated to suit any occasion of the moment. My religion is Caring: but it is not called religion. Caring is all I do. But I care for the individuals and not for something far-off called religious authority. The priests and mullahs can never know the hearts and souls and bodies of these simple and happy people; they do not want to: their prime allegiance is to their religious orders.

"Yes, the Cossacks, whose only care is trade and profit, will use the Czar and the Church as umbrellas under which you gain, gain, gain.

"Your days will go. You are the first pathfinders leading to the first locusts. Then the Church will oust you. Then the Czar will oust the Church. Then the Government will oust the Czar. Then a new Government will oust the old Government. And ever more so.

"We are happy now. Our life is a peaceful ideal. If you stay you are the precursors of a plague. Plague after plague.

"If you return on your road and turn right by seven larch trees instead of left you will reach in twenty miles districts less prosperous, less content, more suited to your kind. They are Bashkirs and are greedy and you can play counter.

"Leave us."

Budar was putting out his incense. He had invited no conversation and no questions.

158

67

Next morning Boris said to Petr: "Let's hurry away. There's syphilis and anthrax here. The commune will be decimated in a year. And dead in two. We should go back till we find seven larches at a division of the roads, then ride south."

Petr looked dubious but Boris allowed him no time for enquiries and they did that.

Boris in the next days achieved all that was expected of him, and he took out his map, bent the prong on his fork, and marked out his venues of conquests for all Cossacks, good and bad, to see.

68

Streltzi was voracious for the division of the spoils, and it took place even before eating upon the party's return to Kormilovka.

If Streltzi was satisfied he didn't show it. Boris felt that as a new-boy he had done well. He took some bales of hides to his room and, pride of all, a sensational sable. Many sales of early winnings had been effected on the markets and Boris was assured that money would be his at any branch of the State Bank.

Boris had feigned a violent stomach complaint and delayed the party's return to Kormilovka till a Saturday as had been Sergei's request.

On arrival Sergei told him it would be announced next day that it was his Names' Day* and that a group were riding out from Omsk to help him celebrate it.

At noon on the Sunday twenty horsemen suddenly burst upon the quiet. There was shooting in the air: shouting, jollity, noise, hilarity galore.

"Your Names' Day!" Sergei burst out. "They've ridden out from Omsk to greet you! Come!"

The horsemen had remained at the gates. Boris and Sergei went out to join them. The Cossacks had instinctively grabbed their guns, but, beyond that, were stunned, and stayed glued to their spots.

Then two hundred horsemen were seen, waiting at the outer fences, all cheering the astonished Boris, in festive mood.

Streltzi and Yakov were alert: bewildered: yet stuck like statues in niches.

Boris was amazed to find Poogavitsa waiting there! and saddled up! Kukurooza too! "Come, mount!" cried Sergei. And Boris, now bewildered himself, did so. Amidst an unholy din the two hundred rode off with the Russian pair.

Someone came alongside Boris. "Our friends cleared out your room and all your loot and belongings are with us."

So Boris had left Kormilovka knowing nothing about it.

He searched out Sergei. "What is happening?"

Sergei said: "It is eighteen miles to the station. We are travelling First Class on the Trans-Siberian Express to Chita."

"First Class?"

"Had to. They wouldn't take our horses on the train unless we travelled First Class, and our animal friends

* Names Day: a day when all of the same name as Ivan, Mitya, Boris, Peter etc. celebrate.

160

were to go with us. But then I thought, why? We won't need them with us in the winter in Chita and I'll be coming back in this direction next summer, so I am leaving Kukurooza here. How about Poogavitsa? Take him with you if you like. But the pair had good quarters together here last winter, and Dr. Yusopoff and Radek will watch over them. So, what do you say, Poogavitsa's booked on the train, but he might be more happy here."

"Yes," said Boris. "If you'll get me back to join him?"

"I will."

69

The great train was in and Boris and Sergei were in it.

Twenty Cossacks with Streltzi and Yakov at the lead entered the station yard. They were firing their guns and rode straight at the engine. They ordered the train to be stopped.

The drivers referred the Cossacks to the Captain. The Captain of the train was positioned exactly centrally. Streltzi and Yakov rode to him. The train was not to leave. There had been a robbery and the robbers were aboard, Yakov shouted.

The Captain calmly said that he could not hold the train for more than the scheduled minutes, where were these robbers? A member of the Omsk posse rode up and said they were in the front carriages and he could lead them to them.

Sergei and Boris watched from their rear carriage.

There was fuss and muddle and upheaval in the front and the Captain informed Streltzi that the train was leaving.

161

"We are the authority in Kormilovka, in the Tiulanisk Region," thundered Streltzi. "You will stay here as long as we tell you to!!"

"You may be the authority in Kormilovka, but I am the authority on this train. Kindly get your men off from the tracks."

There was a flare up which two hundred horsemen from Omsk moulded into a chaos. "They've found your men!" burst out someone to Streltzi. "Two of them, isn't that right? They're taking them off the train now." Two Cossacks who had boarded the train to search for the robbers were being rudely bundled off.

The Captain blew his whistle, calm as ever. The engine blew its whistle and edged out. Streltzi in a rage pulled his gun on the Captain but an Omsk arm nudged it and the bullet only grazed the Captain's leg. The Captain, at last in a fury, blew his whistle so that half the earth and all the sky trembled.

Sergei and Boris gave Streltzi and Yakov a wave as the train moved past them on the platform.

So the great Trans-Siberian left the Cossacks of Kormilovka a-flounder: or, put another way, the Lord of the Land left the ants in their nest in disarray.

70

"Why was Kormilovka station eighteen miles from Kormilovka?" asked Boris.

"So. No stop on the Trans-Siberian goes to where it says it does. Taiga, which means 'in the woods' is well-named: it is the stop for the Capital, Tobolsk, fifty miles from it. Uh. Huh. So."

162

"But why?"

Siberia seemed vaster from the train that it had even seemed from horseback. The landscape was exploding all the time, a one becoming a whole: thus a field strained out to shake hands with the horizon, or a sudden birch forest filled up all space, or the sky became a lid over all it encompassed.

"Because the engineers who planned the line wanted inducements to take the train to a city. Tobolsk pooh-poohed the idea that it should pay to have the train go to the Capital, so the engineers discovered too much hard rock and impassable shale in the way and turned away from Tobolsk fifty miles before it, and veered east and for the fun called the station Taiga, 'in the woods'. Then Tobolsk paid up too late so a branch-line went to within five miles. The engineers wanted more money and never got it. So. Then after another a-do another branch-line went round the city but they never managed to get one through it. So. Now it seems Tobolsk won't be Capital for much longer. So. Kormilovka didn't pay enough."

There was a little face at the door. A little girl. She slid the carriage door open a few inches, tilted her head on one side and stared at the friends.

It was Boris who said, "Hallo."

There was no answer so Boris pursued: "Would you like to come in?" The little girl in a yellow frock showed that she'd like to come in, but she didn't.

"What is your name?"

"Daddy says I'm Valentina, but Mummy says I'm Valenchika."

"How old are you?"

"Daddy says I'm five, but Mummy says I'm nearly six because she had me nine months before Daddy."

"Would you like to come in?"

"Daddy says I shouldn't, but Mummy says I can play

games with some people, but some people might not like it."

"We'll like your game," said Boris. "What is it?"

"Noses."

"What's noses?"

"We have to rub up and down, shall I show you?"

And little Valentina came in at last, climbed on Boris's lap and rubbed her nose crossways and upways against his. Then she climbed down, said "Bye" and was gone.

"The ladies like you," said Sergei.

"Many women like my nose," smiled Boris. And he caressed his nose a little. "I liked Valentina's," he added.

A German came in and wanted to talk about harvesters. Harvesters bored Boris so Boris hoped Sergei would take the brunt of the attack but, alas, the German was followed by another nursing a chess-board and Sergei became an instant lost soul. The two of them settled into a game as if it had all been arranged months before and Boris said to himself 'That's lost Sergei till Chita. And the pair haven't even exchanged names yet! I wonder if they'll find out half way through that they can't speak the same language?'

So Boris got cornered and found out that Siberia evidently was made for harvesters: in fact harvesters and Siberia were synonymous. The only catch was that the Siberians preferred ploughshares: that way they could have a little conversation as they worked. Point out the fact that if they could settle down to harvesters they'd end up with many times the amount of leisure for conversation was a point they couldn't grasp. Harvesters meant loss of conversation-time: though they never explained it that way: the truth, they said, was that harvesters were not suitable for Siberia.

The German drifted on and the vodka got consumed.

Boris noticed that because of the vastness of the landscape, little things became so poignant. An empty countryside with one lone hut, six geese and a cow: and it spoke all toil. A steppe of sedge and reeds and a stream meandering, and a heron explodes into the air, and all life is there in one live heron. . . Boris hoped he was saying the necessary 'I quite agree. . .' 'certainly. . .' 'oh, I think so. . .' but whatever he was saying he had long since exhausted his interest in harvesters.

Sergei said "Good move!" and Boris wondered if he could show some interest in chess, but the German in front of him — neat as a pin in black with a white waistcoat, butterfly collar, smart as a banker in Bonn — said: "Come now, I've had my say: what do you think about it all? Tell me now!" And 'I certainly agree,' or 'definitely not,' didn't fill the blanks any more.

Valentina saved him! Oh dear, sweet Valentina, sent down by the gods in answer to Boris's prayers. . .

"Yes, Valentina?"

"Daddy says it's all right if you like to take me to church."

And the German, Herr Goldstein, who made a point of being informed on everything, solved that one. It would seem that at the next station a Church Car, attached to the train when the Royal Family was on it, was resting in a siding and the Captain had agreed to allow passengers fifteen minutes extra to visit it. So what the Cossacks of Kormilovka hadn't got out of the Captain, God had achieved.

71

The train stopped. Boris saw that the First Class had red carriages, the Second Class blue, and the Third Class green. . . But the little hand was pulling him to Siding Three where the Church Car rested.

It was complete! An absolute church on wheels. There were the ikons, the man-height candlesticks, the brass prayer-stands, carpets, carvings, ornate decorations in gilded wood. A person had to go outside to believe it was merely the width of a railroad track. It *was* a church. Valentina stood with her mouth agape as if waiting for a butterfly to fly in. Her hand was tight in Boris's. Shall I ask her to marry me? he thought, looking down.

The bell went for the train to leave and the lovers had to make a run for it and Boris had been saved from bigamy by the bell.

72

The train squeaked and squealed across the plains. The train was a blood cell running along the artery of this vast land.

The two-berth compartment had cut-glass doors, it had heavy brass fittings, antimacassars, lace curtains, plum coloured carpets, it was musty, comfy, had carmine shaded lamps, it had fat leather chairs as well as bunks, it was all snuggery and had a decorated ceiling arched like the top of grandmama's trunk.

Tea was brought every two hours by a singing attendant called Pasha. She had a little cabin with a big samovar at the end of the carriage.

Certainly Boris must bring Zjennia on such a journey.

But for the moment Zjennia's rival appeared once more at the sliding door pretending to be too shy to come in and with her head aslant on one side.

Then she came in and whispered in Boris's ear. Would he go out to the corridor?

"Yes, Valentina?"

"I want to show you something."

They went past three doors. Valentina stopped. "Look."

"What at?"

"That nose."

"Which one?"

"The third on the left."

A nose like a banana.

Like a curved elongated syringe. No, like a banana.

"You want to play with it?"

"I love it."

"Leave it to me."

Valentina had a strange passion. But then, it was true, who ever saw a banana for a nose before?

Boris asked if he could speak with the owner of that unique possession. The man rose. Abram was his name.

"You might not believe this," Boris began. "But a young lady has fallen in love with you. She's very young. A dear little thing of five. And you mustn't ask me why, she wants to meet you. And she's very, very shy. Why not please a little tiny girl and come and say 'hallo'?"

"Are you her father?"

"No. Just a friend of the train. We'll ask her about her

167

father. A nice little thing. Valentina is her name. Will you come?"

"Of course."

Boris went first. "I didn't say a word about his banana," he whispered to Valentina. "I just asked him to meet you. He's coming."

And Boris introduced Abram who, though correct and proper, was flattered.

So relaxed is the atmosphere in the corridors of the Trans-Siberian Express that such unusual happenings are usual.

"Where is your Daddy?" asked Boris.

"He's there on the right."

And she pointed further on where two men were holding glasses and talking.

"Then I'll go and thank him."

73

The Express moved on into the vastnesses, through this land of cruelty, heartbreak, injustice, of unspeakable cold, of hopelessness, of hell, of tears too inhuman. . . and yet, of a freedom unknown anywhere else in Russia, unknown indeed in most places in the world. Were not Sergei and Boris, two escaped Czarist prisoners, enjoying roaming where they will with never a question asked? Siberia: the great enigma, the great contradiction.

After making a dozen new friends in this warm, snug, well-fed, singing train, as it chig-chug chig-chugged on through one empty space to another empty space, Boris returned to find the last chess-match of the evening just completing and the rest of the compartment vacant.

Boris settled by the carmine-shaded lamp, with the everlasting glass of Russian tea just brought in by the singing Pasha from the ever-steaming samovar and, yes, Valentina stood even again at their door, coyly shame-faced but wanting to be asked in.

She came and climbed on Boris's lap. . . "Not asleep yet?" asked Boris. . . and she wanted to tell him about the Trans-Siberian Express.

"Then what is it?" Boris smiled.

"You should smile more!" said the little girl suddenly strongly. Then she began: "If you go to the railway tracks outside Moscow and stare down the way of the Trans-Siberian Express the lines get" (and she shouted) "smaller" (and she shouted a little less) "and smaller" (and she gave an ordinary shout) "and smaller" then a shout-whisper "and smaller" then down and down till even the whispers died away "and smaller, and smaller" and when he could hear her no more, she nodded forward and was asleep against his chest.

"I will smile more," he said, and stroked her hair.

The seventeen-carriage bore of the Express drilled on through the jowls of the night. Siberia, now graveyard quiet, trees stark still, steppes deserted as death, a rare farm hut with its dark cloak pulled round it, the carriage wheels so frightened at their own click-clack that their echoes scurried back to rejoin the train to follow it to Chita. Past Ulan Udz and Petrovski Zavod, past Zaigraevo and Bada. At Kharagun shawl-shadows stood out, and in a pond, infinity was drinking a thousand stars. Sergei opened a window and threw out a cigarette, the wind from the opened window stage-whispered of escape stories, then Sergei closed the window on the escapes and came and patted the little girl's head and returned to look at the chess-board, Valentina, slugged

169

by a capsule of eternity, fast asleep in Boris's lap and Boris vowing he must have a daughter, and the train writhing on into the void, an anaconda into the black.

74

Next morning, singing Pasha had brought the friends tea, and they were by the window.

"I'm asking the Czar for a pardon," said Sergei.

"Have you a chance?" asked Boris astonished.

"It's not what your crime was. If you've committed a hundred murders or stolen a chicken, that's the same. It's if you know someone near the top to whom you can offer a fancy prize. Yermak offered all the lands he had conquered east of the Urals, and the generous offer was exchanged for a mean pardon. I have built up an immense network of communications. I will tell you about it one day. I can hand over the title-deeds. I can offer at least. Who knows?"

"Baikal!!" The shout went up from the corridors. There was a rush to the outside windows as the cry ran down the train like a flame down a fuse.

Sergei went over to the chess-board and handled a piece. He put it down and went to Boris who was already leaving for the corridor.

"How much does your freedom mean to you? Your freedom to go home? Sergei asked.

Boris stopped in his tracks.

"It would mean the life-line to my life."

Sergei picked up another chess piece and turned it around, then put it down again.

"I'll ask for you as well. I'll say you are my partner."

A gang rushed in and dragged them to the corridor.

The hills were crowding in, pressing against the windows: then there was a split in the hills, a rift, and the lake was there, twenty million dancing diamonds flashing up from the waters and half blinding the passengers.

Such phantasmagoria skinned the mind. Here was the world's greatest lake. More water here than in the whole Baltic Sea, England could be buried in it, in length; and buried under it, in depth. An aeon older than Man: to Baikal the dinosaur was yesterday: with eight hundred species of flora and fauna known nowhere else on earth.

Boris must find Sergei.

A lake fed by three hundred and thirty-three rivers and emptied only by one, the raging Angara. Encased by the Maritime Range, by the Baikalsky Range and the Khamar-Daban range: the home of the wolverene, the stag, the boar, the sable, the eagle and the swan.

Boris found Sergei. He clutched at him. "You think you can help me about the pardon?"

"I will try. We'll try together. So. Enjoy Baikal."

Where is little Valentina? Your Boris is smiling now! And the smile is permanent.

Baikal was itself. Untouched by the festers of man: by hotels, by camps, by factories. Siberia's greatest miracle. At 200 feet down, iron railway lines can be twisted out of recognition by the pressures, yet at a 1000 feet down the little twelve-inch golumanya fish can resist all pressure in spite of its no bone structure. Bring it to the surface and 'pop' it's little more than a few drops of moisture in the hand. Ducks fly in daily 100 miles to feed and fly 100 miles back again to sleep. The Ice Age retreated so quickly from here that the seals never got away and breed still on the northern shore two thousand miles from the open sea. 7000 are harpooned every year and yet the population remains static. Those seals can see for more than a mile so hunters have to be clever at their own camouflage. Sturgeons four feet long live a hundred years here and, for their twenty year fertile period, they are taken out, milked for their caviare and placed back in.

"There's the entrance to the Angara River there," said Sergei. "Have you heard of the Sharman Rock?"

Boris had heard Sergei's previous sentence about 'pardons' and was mentally breaking the news to Zjennia, but he hadn't heard of the Sharman so "What is that?" he asked.

"So. Criminals are chained to it with their hands behind their backs. If they drown it means they were innocent and will reach Paradise; if they escape and don't drown that means they were guilty and must have their throats cut. So."

The Ice Age was yesterday here. The pterodactyl scarcely out of sight. Silence was here before death. When a storm breaks here, Baikal doesn't play with the ship, it splinters it and tosses it up on the rocks. When a volcano erupts beneath its surface, it can smash out ten miles of near land and give birth to a new lake. Fishermen live here, but live in awe. Yet they worship the lake.

The train came down from the heights and curled now with the curve of the waters.

Boris's and Sergei's had been the only voices by the windows. Now they too were silent.

Twenty million years old.

Yes, silence is the only conversation at Baikal.

172

75

"Sergei!"

"Radakov!"

And two old friends had met and embraced in warm Russian style.

It was on the Irkutsk platform.

A vision passed by. A slender reed in silver grey taffeta with her dress nearly down to her toes. Boris stood transfixed and could scarcely force himself back to reality to meet Radakov. "My oldest business friend from Chita," Sergei was saying. "You are going to Chita now?" he asked.

"Oh yes. But I must see about the baggage," said Radakov.

And Boris hurried down the platform to get another glance at the vision. It was something from another world. Russia was a coarse country. Siberia was coarser. What he had seen was fresh, elegant, stately, and, why that stupid word, 'clean'? A clean stalk in a grubby world. Where the hell was she? The down train was going and he couldn't spot her. One more glance, that's all he wanted. One more glance was not much to ask.

The train *was* starting and he just jumped on before the steps did their disappearing act retracting underneath the waggons – perhaps designed to stop the likes of him or brodyagis boarding the train in full flight.

That vision, and the fact that he had not caught a second glimpse, would haunt Boris now. He had heard of – wasn't it Dante? – who had caught a sight of Beatrice which had stayed in his mind till the end of his days– Boris had had a glance at his Beatrice.

Radakov came in. A stately man, just less than middle-aged, a ladies'-man for certain. Boris was not surprised to find he had been a soldier.

"Ah!" said Radakov. "My daughter."

The vision stood before them.

"Natalya, gentlemen."

Boris knew he behaved as if stunned. What could he do? He *was* stunned.

Nineteen? Twenty? Perhaps nineteen. Hazel eyes. How strange, Zjennia had hazel eyes too: perhaps with more honey in them. But there wasn't another thing that was similar. When he thought of Zjennia, he only wanted to ravish her. Here was a vision beyond the thought of ravishing.

Radakov and Sergei were lost in talk. So Boris had to open up with the vision.

"Will you sit?" he asked.

"Thank you." And she did.

"Are you alive?" he asked. "There's something unreal about you. You must be the single most beautiful person who has ever lived."

She knit her brows a little. "What can I say? You don't have to be gallant."

"Gallant? I'm not being gallant. You leave me not being myself. But I will try. It wouldn't do if I appeared to you as an idiot, would it? I will try to come back to earth. Are you of the earth?"

"Very much."

"Then I will try to join you there. You are not Russian, are you?"

"My father is Russian. My mother is American. I live in Pennsylvania."

"That's terrible: so far away. You are only visiting?"

"I visit here often. Father's work is with trade between the countries. Mother doesn't like to come much. So I come. And I will come in the future. What do you do?"

174

"I follow Sergei at the moment. And I am following him to Chita. I will work with him there."

"He's one of my father's most admired friends."

Pasha came in. Humming.

"This is Pasha," said Boris. "She's humming now. But she's usually singing. Pasha, have you a silver holder for a glass of tea for Natalya Radakova here?"

"I love 'Natalya', said Pasha. "Like 'Natasha' in 'War and Peace'. She is my favourite. Because of her I think all Natalyas and Natashas are from a dream world. She shall have the best holder I can find, sir."

Natalya had an imp which charmed, a youthfulness which charmed, a poetry-voice which charmed. She smiled up from within herself as if someone nice was talking to her inside. She was a pixie groomed in elegance.

Boris was lost.

76

The train seemed to stop almost as soon as it had started. It had actually travelled forty-six miles but in the frame of mind that Boris was in distance and time shrank to zero.

It was 'everybody out'.

The train was to load on to its ferry at Baranchuk and Baikal was to be crossed for the train to re-start at Mysovaya.

The four remained together, walked together, talked together, watched together and remained inseparable.

"What a great ship this is," said Radakov. "Made in England. There you can see it, 'Armstrong, Whitworth &

Co. Newcastle', isn't it? Then it was taken to pieces, sent here in bits and, with engineers and workers mainly from St. Petersburg, it was re-assembled like a jig-saw in two years. Zablotsky, you know him Sergei?, was the engineer who put it together. It has been faultless since. It's an ice-breaker, but used in the summer too. In the winter it breaks the ice to the depth of four feet. The total thickness of the ice on Baikal is nine and a half feet. Did you know that in the lowest depths of the lake the temperature doesn't vary the whole year round and is a constant three above zero?"

"Was it worth all that effort to have it built in England and brought out?"

"Oh yes. They've just made the second one too, to be called the 'Angara'. But the Russians are attempting the third one themselves, under German supervision. The English deserved something out of it, anyhow."

"Why?"

"Why? Why, this whole idea, this Trans Siberian Railway was a British idea. After an engineer, Mr. Dull, had failed to get his plans for a horse-train accepted, three other English, Morison, Sleigh and Horn in 1858 followed it up and pressed for the railway. But they too were turned down. So we decided to discover the idea ourselves and built all this. This is the last hiccough to surmount, this ferry lift on Baikal, but this too will be cleared up soon."

"They are bringing the train on."

"The same people, Armstrong, Whitworth & Co. made the 'Fram' for Nansen to go to the North and South Pole. The 'Fram' is awfully like this ship here."

There were three pairs of railway lines set along the axis of the ship and twenty-five loaded waggons were drawn on to the main deck. On the upper deck were places for 800 passengers and cabins for 150.

There was much to be wondered at in the activity.

Radakov did most of the talking. Sergei most of the
listening. Natalya most of the musing. Boris most of the
dreaming.

77

"Do you like it in Siberia?" Boris
asked Natalya.

"No. Do you?"

"I like it now. Yes, I like it. But now especially.
Pennsylvania, is that much better?"

"Come and see," Natalya said.

"Are you inviting me?"

"Yes. I invite you."

"Then tell me why you prefer it."

"It is clean. It has little poverty. It is warmer. It has
beautiful trees and houses. The men don't smell like
horses as they do here. And the people try to make it
nice. No one tries here."

"Yet you come?"

"Father always likes Mother or me to come. It was my
turn. Father likes it here in a way. It's part of him I
suppose. I have no Russian in me, except very very
deep. On the surface I love clean places. I hate poverty. I
hate suffering."

"And deep deep down?"

"And deep deep down? You have soul here. And
nothing else. In Pennsylvania we have everything else.
And no soul."

"And if I come to see you, in Pennsylvania, shall I
bring my soul with me?"

"Don't you dare come without it!"

177

78

The young Captain of the 'Baikal' invited Radakov and his daughter to the Captain's table for dinner that evening, and Boris was out in the cold.

The young Captain gave Natalya all possible attention before and after dinner as well, and all Boris could do was to console himself with thinking that soon the ship would be left and it would be back to the social rounds of the train.

But that was not to be, for the Captain found reasons for joining the train and deserting his ship, and Boris, who had thought he might as well be generous since it was all so temporary and had proffered compliments about the Captain to Natalya, now wished he had kept the sugar off his tongue.

He fought for all the openings he could but Natalya was a new species to him: he had never met a woman with such assurance, she gave the feeling that the world was hers and as if the world was a chess-board with she the power behind the moves. She never rebuffed Boris, but she seemed to fit him in to the empty spaces available and she never sought him out.

Radakov and his daughter were the two most sought after on the journey and they played it that way, but graciously.

Other male suitors for Natalya appeared from nowhere: the train got full of them and Boris got full of murder. After a tentative outburst of jealousy, the charmer Natalya, looking immaculate as snow, left him with an instant feeling that he'd be crossed off the list altogether if he persevered with that line. She was an angel with spurs.

A freak happening came to his aid. He and Sergei had drifted in to a musical compartment. Even Pasha had come and proudly sang: then left to attend to her samovar. Boris had asked for the balalaika and sang three songs. The Captain and Natalya passed the door and listened. The whole compartment hummed in accompaniment.

Boris saw her alight in white silk, slender as a willow bough.

"I'm sorry," he said.

"Sorry?" she asked. She came and sat on the edge of his seat beside him. "Why are you sorry?"

"I did not know you were there."

"Even the stars came down to listen," she said. "We need that soul in Pennsylvania. Do come. But bring your own balalaika. That's just the two things we haven't got there: balalaikas and souls."

79

Boris looked forward to Chita where Natalya would be staying with her father and the Captain would have returned to the 'Baikal'.

But the Captain did not return to his ship, and excuses got grander and grander, from being transferred to a cargo ship on the Baltic to being made Captain of the Czarist Navy's latest dreadnought at Vladivostock. He disappeared out of town from time to time but constantly turned up again. Once he met Natalya and Boris at a street corner. Boris, who haunted Natalya's home and pounded the snows around it to brown slush daily, managed that way to meet his beloved three times a week with an 'Oh, it's you. Fancy meeting you coming this way.' It was at one such meeting that the young Captain, always unfairly resplendent in uniform, spotted them and invited Natalya to visit a garden. Since winter was bitingly upon them, the garden needed explanation. An Admiral Chirkov, retired, had discovered among the rocks on his estate a corner where the winter sun reached and the winter winds didn't, bringing forth freak, exciting tiny flowers, and he, the Captain, could get permission to show her.

Natalya accepted for both of them. "We'd like to come, wouldn't we, Boris?" Which answer affected both men with opposing emotions. But it pleased Boris so much that he decided that this corner of Ladies Street where they were now standing was his lucky spot. Ladies Street was named after the Princesses Volkonskoya and Trubetskoya who had followed their princely husbands into exile as Decembrists and had regular rendezvous with each other just at this point.

The Captain added that wolves were worrying visitors to the gardens, but it should be clear.

And the three risked it.

They had reached the endearing tiny Arctic flowers when the Captain suddenly shouted "Wolves!" and vanished.

And three wolves appeared. Boris was able to snap off a sturdy willow branch and kept springing in front of Natalya as one set of snarling teeth appeared after another. Three of them were hard to keep at bay. Boris told Natalya to move slowly back along the path that they had come down. Of all ridiculous things in such an out-of-place circumstance he suddenly reflected that her breasts – now hiding under a mountain of fur – were twin cups of alabaster.

180

She did as he asked, and controlled her fears. Boris lashed and slashed and rounded her in crazy circles and pace by pace they edged towards the gate where they had entered. The Captain was at the gate, on the safe side of the fence and, as the pair came close, thrust the gate open with a swing.

They were through and it was Boris who closed it, the Captain already off with Natalya explaining how he had reacted quickly and hurried to have the gate open to enable them to escape quickly. "It was quick thinking, but I had to act like lightning to do the best for everyone."

Boris felt proud and thought he must have put paid to the Captain's attentions towards Natalya forever. It was too, too obvious, that if someone had put his body in front of Natalya to protect her, who that someone was.

But, beyond all reasoning, Natalya fell more for the heroic words of the Captain than for the ludicrous actions of her protector. Boris made no comment, certain that with hindsight she would soon realise where value lay. But she never did. Boris recounted the incident to Sergei. "So," said Sergei. "Heroic words win more disciples than heroic actions. So."

A month later the Captain left and never came back. Natalya said little of it, but Boris knew that whatever had been between them, was over for all time.

80

On a walk round the snow-carpeted streets Natalya said: "Did Sergei tell you why my father is forever grateful to him?"

Boris said: "Sergei would never say why anybody is grateful to him. He never mentions such things."

"My father was not rich but he was working on the Amur when some information about a Chinese and Russian future deal passed his ears: that is, that he should not have learnt of it, at the same time it was no sin or crime that he did so: he just 'happened' to learn of it: it was a freak chance. But there was a fortune in it if he could get the news to powerful friends in St. Petersburg. He went to Sergei. One of Sergei's systems works like this: he and my father put it in a code that only one friend in St. Petersburg could break. They'll never forget that message because of the funny rhyme it added up to. It's cold isn't it? Can we turn here to get out of the wind?"

"No," said Boris. "There's a little Italian shop one street on and we can buy coffee there. It's called 'Chita'. Did you know that this town 'Chita' is named after an Italian?"

And they hurried to the shop through the swirling wind.

Then Natalya continued. . . "Oh yes," said Boris first, "the funny rhyme?". . . "The funny rhyme was. . ." 'God!' felt Boris, 'something destroys me in her: it's not just the beauty, it's not just the elegance, something in that puckishness. . . how can a simple thing like that destroy a man?' He scarcely heard the rhyme, but managed "Once more" and she repeated: "'The Ging of England git appears, gas not gad beer for twenty years'."

Then Natalya went on: "Sergei called five friends together and gave it to one of them. The other four did not know to which. But each of the five had five friends each and the one who received the message gave it to one of his five. Then it went on in fives throughout Chita, Siberia, Russia, so if anybody such as the militia or Czarist police were on to it you will see from mathematics

182

the net would soon grow into thousands, even into hundreds of thousands, and no one could keep checks on such a number. Eventually the message reached St. Petersburg, my father's friends jumped into action, and in less than six months my father jumped from an ordinary wealthy man to an extraordinary wealthy man. So now you know why, since Sergei and my father both asked me if I would show more friendliness to you. . ."

"You. . . all these meetings. . . all this. . . is just because Sergei and your father. . . Bill, please! Bring me the bill!!"

Boris was raging. He would not let Natalya in with a word. He had grown to a volcano in seconds. "Just because. . . oh Christ! Oh Christ! Well. . . There's your bill, keep the change! Excuse me, Natalya, I must go!!"

"The man is mad," said Natalya to herself.

So all these meetings, he said to himself, all this pretence at friendship, was just because Sergei, damn him, and her father, damn him, had asked her. . .

How Boris got through the rest of that day he will never know.

81

Next morning there was a knock at Boris's door. Natalya was shown in.

She stood by the door and would not come in further.

Boris was seated.

She said: "An Uzbek poet, Paklavan Makmud, who lived not all that very far from here nearly six hundred years ago wrote:

'To go through a hundred mountains
To be locked up in the jail for a hundred years
To colour the sky with the blood of your heart
Is easier than to speak to a stupid man.'

"I am lowering myself for the first, and I hope the last, time in my life to speak to such a stupid man. What I told you yesterday about Sergei and my father was a conversation piece only. A story to tell as we took time and coffee together. If I had not wanted to meet you, to speak with you, then a hundred Sergeis and a thousand fathers would not have got me to. Your behaviour showed no soul that I want to know. Tomorrow at twelve noon I'll be at our usual corner in Ladies Street. If you are there, you are there. If you are not there, then you are not there."

She turned to go.

"Natalya, one moment. . ."

She paused.

"I'll be there," he said.

82

There were sleigh rides in the woods. There were parties at which Boris hated trying to be a gentleman. There were the meetings at street corners which became rendezvous and not chance meetings.

And more sleigh rides, with dog teams, with reindeer and with troika horses.

The couple met more and more and more. She still exuded that tom-boy kittenishness which was melting. Yet she had inexplicable moments of frigidity, and went into a stiff aloof assurance mood which was baffling and beyond Boris's power to thaw. She would not admit the moods' existence and came out of such peevish coldness slowly or suddenly equally inexplicably.

But, though suitors were never absent, Boris had more and more of the time of this smiling hyacinth who, even after months, still left him with a feeling of that odd adjective 'clean'. Chita was rough, tough, Arctic cold and, whenever it got the chance, as filthy as a rat's paradise. Even Boris at home, to escape the bugs in his bedroom had to pull out his bed into the centre, then surround it with insect powder, then, the bugs, not to be defeated, climbed the walls and along the ceiling until they could drop on him in a pin-point nose-dive from on high. Thereafter he had to line all round the base of the walls with more powder. Out-of-doors it was merciful that the temperature was an ever well-under-zero so that what bug-life and rat-life the town exuded was forced to stay indoors.

And here, set in all this, was this Russian-American miracle disarmingly, unnervingly, magnetically 'clean'. Boris spruced himself up till he was hardly Boris any more, not at her request but from a feeling that it would be wrong to accompany her otherwise.

83

Natalya overwhelmed Boris in the best of possible ways.

And Boris knew what he had to do.

He must propose marriage. He must follow her to America. He must wed her there. All other issues, and Samara, must find their own way into the background.

185

Radakov had gone to Irkutsk. Natalya was alone in the sumptuous house – with servants and without bugs.

Boris suggested he should visit her. She suggested evening.

He bought the largest ruby and the largest emerald he had ever seen, each encased in a gold and enamel casket.

He left. Walking on air.

In the house, a mile outside town, only candles burned. Inside was the first wealthy interior he had seen which was under-furnished, not over-furnished as was the Russian style. The rooms were roomy, and the empty spaces added a sumptuous elegance.

Natalya had a stiff cut snow-drop white blouse. Her long skirt was crocus yellow. Her waist, a few hand-clasps round, was girdled with a silver belt.

Boris could not eat, could not drink. He nibbled and sipped. He could not speak. He took out his gifts, his ruby and emerald, but before he could present them to her, she was called away.

Something clutched him. He rose. Clutched him and would not release him. Clutched him tighter and tighter. Clutched him till he was suffocating at the chest.

Frantically he grabbed the emerald.

He was seized within and without.

He scribbled on a piece of paper 'A jewel for a jewel' and left the ruby burnishing there.

Clutched him at the throat. Clutched again.

"FOR THE LOVE OF ZJENNIA, DAMN HER!!"

Fled headlong from the house.

Never saw Natalya again.

84

The pardons had come. And summer had come. Two reasons for being on the move.

Sergei and Boris were free men! Ten years of toil of building up the most envied communications network 'overground' and 'underground' in the country exchanged for two slips of paper.

"I'll have a drink," said Boris.

"So. Me too," said Sergei.

So they had a drink.

"I'll enjoy seeing Poogavitsa again," said Boris.

"Me too. Seeing Kukurooza. So," said Sergei.

And they had another drink.

"I had a dream last night," said Boris.

"So?" said Sergei.

"That Steltzi was drowning and Yakov threw him out a rope. Both ends of it."

"So!"

"You saved my life. You got me a pardon," said Boris.

"You saved mine. From beneath the snows near Omsk," said Sergei.

"What I did was imperative," said Boris. "What you did was not imperative: an act of salvation."

"What you did," said Sergei, "took some doing! What I did was to add a name."

"If you're going to argue about it!" said Boris. "We'll need another drink!"

So they took another drink.

"I am going to Samara," said Boris.

"I am going to Moscow," said Sergei.

Their legs were getting unsteady.

So, each with a bottle in his hand and another in his pocket, they left for the streets 'To walk it off' they said.

"Off tomorrow," they said. "To Poogoo and Kuku. Off we go."

"So!" agreed Sergei.

They came to a small square, on one side of which was the quayside to a small lake. On the opposite side of the square was a row of small shops, the last one dying into a fence and a field. On the right, looking from the quay, were some stalls and Boris sprawled on a log there. Neither of them can remember what was on the left side, though there must have been another log because Sergei remembered sitting on a log there.

There was no action in the shops. Perhaps it was late.

Boris called across: "Your health!" And Sergei answered "So!" And they had another drink. But something worried them both at the same time. In front of them, well in front of a shop and near the stall on Boris's side, was a man sitting on a chair. The man was very still and had a small glass on the ground beside him. The friends called out "Your health!" but there was no response. No reaction at all.

Boris and Sergei struggled to raise themselves and went to the man. Very motionless.

They filled his glass on the ground. They touched the man on the shoulder to motion to him that they had filled his glass up but with the touch the man fell to the ground. They propped him up again, went back to their places but were puzzled and stared at the chair and the figure.

A man in blue balloon trousers and a long red blouse with sleeves like syringes, appeared just as a stall-owner turned up to close down his stall. The newcomer demanded "Fresh fish! I demand fresh fish!"

188

"You have the wrong stall. I don't sell fish, fresh or otherwise. I sell pots and pans."

"If you don't give me fresh fish, you'll find yourself a corpse here by the morning!"

The man with the blue balloon trousers marched off in high dudgeon.

The stall-owner turned and for the first time noticed the body on the chair, went to it, touched it, it fell. "Corpse already!" he spluttered, and hurried to the quayside. There was a small boat there and the stall-keeper began to pull the body to the boat.

Boris and Sergei struggled to their feet and helped him.

They got the man from the chair into the boat, seated him upright and pushed him out.

The stall-owner, shaking like a leaf and swearing he had been sent an omen, accepted a dram and the friends went back to their places. Then the stall-owner stayed on with Boris and accepted a second drink.

There were cries from the water. "Look out! Look out! Don't come here, I've got my nets out!"

It seemed that the boat was drifting towards a fisherman who had spread out his nets.

The three men on the ground turned just in time to see the fisherman swipe at the body in the boat with an oar, and flatten him. "Oh!" cried the fisherman and pulled the boat alongside to his own and dexterously manoeuvred the two to the shore.

One of the shop-keepers appeared at this time from behind closed doors and left a box outside. He was a bee-keeper and a producer of honey, and had encased a hive to take home, awaiting a boy with a cart. He turned inside the shop to lock up.

Meanwhile the fisherman had reached the shore and struggled to get the body out. "I have killed him! I have killed him!" he kept muttering. It was too great a task for him to drag the body alone so the three men struggled to their feet to help.

They got the body out, yanked it across the square and set it on the chair again. The fisherman accepted a drink and stayed back for a second one, settling on the log near Sergei.

The bee-keeper came out and seeing the body on the chair, went over and asked "Aren't you young Oskar's father? Oskar will be along in a minute with a lineika." He nudged the man who fell to the ground. "My bees have attacked him and killed him!" cried the poor man. "Oh I must not let Oskar see."

And he tried to pull the man away.

The four men struggled to their feet to help him.

On the left of the square the priest's carriage awaited the priest and the horse was enjoying a nosebag of maize.

"Let's put the body near the priest's cart," the beekeeper said. And after a great struggle they did that.

The bee-keeper accepted a drink to calm his agitation and joined Boris and the stall-holder by their log to work out what he would say to Oskar about killing his father.

The priest's horse suddenly made a bolt for it, crashed into a fence, the horse got away, but the cart remained.

The priest had appeared and witnessed the scene and bent over the cart. "Oh my heaven, I have killed a man! What can I do with the body?"

He struggled to get the body up, but it was too much for him, so the five men rose as one from the logs and helped him.

They returned the body to its seat on the chair.

The priest worried how he would explain it to his parishioners and accepted a dram to help him think it out.

He joined Sergei by his log who produced a second bottle from his jacket pocket just as Boris remembered

190

he had brought an extra bottle also in case of emergency. "So!" said Sergei.

The priest remembered he had a coffin in his cart, and they all struggled up and brought the coffin out. They brought it to the chair and laid the body in.

The priest said, it was the custom in Chita always to lay some kumyss alongside a corpse to help it 'to the other side' so they picked up the glass which had been alongside the chair and filled it afresh, asking the priest if God would overlook that it wasn't kumyss? Respect also demanded that a cap covered the head of the dead. The six laid the coffin on the front of the stall and grouped together to discuss where to find a cap. Oskar charged in with his lineika and reared his horse up sharply in the centre of the square.

Young Oskar saw the coffin, said he had no idea who the man was, it was not his father, but it might be an old friend of his mother's who was ill and she had asked him to pick him up but he had got delayed so long and oh dear, look, the delay had killed the man!

So he took off his cap and laid it on the man's head.

Then the youth had a drink to help him think out how he'd explain it to his mother.

And the seven drank till the moon came up and cast its suspicious eye upon the scene.

Then they put the coffin, still open, on to the lineika. Oskar drove off solemnly with the six followers behind.

Some say the corpse sat up and said: "What's this? I'm not dead." And that Oskar said "The priest should know better than you!" and knocked him down again.

Some say the corpse then took the spirit, raised its cap and accepted the ride.

Others say that when they reached the cemetery and went to bury the body, the body wasn't there.

Others say it wasn't the cemetery.

191

Boris and Sergei could never agree on the matter and argued it out for half the journey from Chita to Omsk.

85

Eva was dying. Summer had come and in the winter Eva had married the youth of her dreams, Nikolai, Ch——'s only schoolmaster.

If Zjennia's marriage to Boris had been the explosion of the region, then Eva's and the shy Nikolai's had been the love match for all sweethearts to coo about.

And now, only three months on, Eva was dying.

Popovitch had sent the best doctors from Samara, the priest, Alexis, had talked the Patriarch of Kazan into visiting and giving God's blessings, the doctor, Bogodin, did nothing and knew less but, to his credit, never pretended otherwise, every caring quack for ten miles round had offered a remedy, but nothing unravelled the mystery and Eva sank deeper.

Nikolai had come to Zjennia with an obsessional idea to take Eva two hundred miles north east to Tulayev, a shaman, who had earned himself a notoriety for miracles. Eva, fast losing touch with life, but with her love-bond still strong enough to fight for her Nikolai, had agreed to be taken and three lineikas left Ch—— on a summer's day for the distant north east.

A week later, after many an hour of near despair that all would be too late, the three long carts entered the distant commune.

The night after their arrival would be a new moon and this was auspicious, and even if Nikolai and Zjennia had begged the shaman to try any potions or miracles before, they knew the shaman knew, the local wide world knew, nothing can equal the power of an auspicious omen.

There seemed a merest shadow remaining of Eva and nothing would drag Nikolai away from her. Tulayev, the shaman, therefore received Zjennia alone.

86

Zjennia had had the plan of the house that she was entering explained to her. It was a large log cabin central to the commune. It was raised half a floor only and nothing was kept below. Half a flight of steps led to a sumptuous square room. There were no stools or chairs. The floor was of birch twigs, overladen with thick furs and skins, mostly elk and deer and bear. Zjennia found it easier for the tread than she had supposed. There were strips of silver birch bark dividing the floor in two. Into one half visitors could be received. The other half was for the shaman only, or for his servants who attended bare-footed, and no one must cross that line unless invited by the shaman himself. There were also four other smaller divisions, also marked by strips of less wide birch bark. There was a bedroom, a servants room, a preparatory kitchen and a general room. Although the divisions were imaginary – just those strips of birch bark – Zjennia had only been present a few minutes before she felt them as real as the stoutest walls.

In the exact centre was a fire, ánd above the fire an opening in the roof which, at two hands-widths above it, had a large iron hood, which could be brought down to seal the hole if wished. But while the heat rising up was greater than the draught coming down, this was not necessary. The huge pots in the centre above the everlasting fire could thus serve both guest and host on either side of the main division of the room.

Zjennia seated herself opposite the shaman.

"There are more cushions behind you," he said.

She felt utterly snug and could not believe the comfort of the floor.

But Tulayev surprised her. He neither had a powerful form, nor head. He was more frail than strong. He looked ageless but might be thirty.

"You are Hungarian," he said.

She sat up sharply.

"My mother and father both came from Hungary. I was only four. No one has remarked on our origin before."

"You are at home," he said.

"How do you mean?" This man rattled her. Her usually soft and silky voice had become purposeful in tone.

"This spot and the whole area here around was the home of the Hungarians. The Bulgars came from nearer Samara. Your Samara area was named Bulgar till the 14th century. Your two peoples emigrated and stopped side by side together again by the Danube. You followed the curve of the Milky Way — Hadakuttya in Hungarian. It's the path the swans, the ducks, the geese take every year. Your word means 'The Way of the Armies'. Doh, who was the first Hungarian shaman, fled to the sun up the Milky Way and made it visible. By the Danube you were forced into Christianity. Your famous King Stephen forced Thomuzola, the last shaman, to be buried alive alongside his alive wife at Fort Abad: your famous King Bela IV had the last shamaness, Usihana, confined until she had eaten her own feet, then he left

194

her to die in the same spot. Each did it because they said shamans were heathen."

"Does this mean you will treat my Christian sister badly in revenge?"

He looked at her darkly. There was a long silence.

"I beg you, forgive me," she said. "Some Christians in Ch——had said it would be so."

The silence persisted. He then spoke quietly as if he did not like saying what he was saying: "Men transfer the evil that is in them onto others. Thus a thief will have it that all men are thieves, a liar that all men lie, a boaster that all men boast. We anoint our enemies with our own evils. Thus did the Christian kings."

It was the first time in her life she had apologised to any man. Did he know he was the first to lower her pride?

"You are proud," he said. "It was the Tungus who gave you the name Magyar. Magyar means proud and fiery. You have points of metal in your bearing and are haughty like star points, though you coat it round in an insatiable warmth. You glow as if your veins run lightning. And are beautiful as morning. I have a present for you."

He took out from beneath his clothes a button.

"This I found when walking in the woods. It is a Hungarian button of a thousand years ago. Accept it from me."

She put her hand out and their hands met over the birch bark.

"Why are you dressed as a woman?" she asked.

"I must be all things to all people. All here know I am a man. Therefore I dress as a woman to show that I know of women also. There is an odd physical happening to me for putting on women's clothes. Dressed as male I am strong, but docile. Dressed as woman I am strong, but forceful. I don't understand that. All people here, and children too, expect much from me. I have to enter into them, into their concerns and sicknesses. And tomorrow I have to enter into your sister. Will you drink tea or spirit?"

"Tea."

"It will be Tungus tea. With both honey and fats in it."

Tea was brought but he had none. "I must not drink," he said. "Tomorrow I walk on burning aspen, and I imbibe fire. I have not drunk for three days. If I have no liquid in me, it is easier to walk on fire."

"Why do you do such things?"

Again he looked at her darkly. Again there was a lengthy silence. Again he spoke quietly as if he did not want to bring the words out. "The thirst for delusion is the bane of the universe. It is a pity so. But belief is the great healer. And miracles are the shortest cut to earn believers. My people must believe in me. So I walk on fire. A miracle to them. Delusion to you and me. But my Hungarian Zjennia, be warned! I must tell you: delusion or not, believe in belief! It's a very great secret. And with your sister too. Nikolai must get it into her that she has returned to the home of her ancestors and that this is auspicious. That it is a new moon. And that that is auspicious. And that we will use the Hungarian drum which is of doe-skin on birch. She must believe. It is at the root of things."

"Do you believe?"

"I believe in belief. Drink your tea. You shall have Russian tea if you prefer it. At least three time a week I leave my body. It is a technique. A cruel thing. Others do not realise how I am not so much of this world, and how I lose by it. I must visit the source of sicknesses, I must wander far over the Yenesei and Volga, I must visit the future to find if a woman will bear a child, I wander, wander, through this world and through outer worlds, that these my people shall know when the rains will

196

come, when the winds will blow the reindeer scent here, when locusts will come. . . oh, my Samara friend, Zjennia, how can I break it to my people that three years from now half of them will be dead from famine? And famine will ravish your Samara region also. I can warn you: but how can I warn them? We live our life in the mirror, did you know that? It's for me to look in the mirror before, or sometimes after, an event. It is easy to know the future weather. I know the symptoms physically. Have you noticed that no Tungus will ever ask the way? They retain the instinct of the birds. But many things they do not retain. Their everyday life eats their time. So I am their thermometer, see-er — their looker in the mirror of life. Will you come and sit beside me? Just come over the birch bark. It is very easy. I will hold out my hand. You could warm us all through the coldest winter. You are imperious, but never to the meek. How I am enlightened to be with a true Magyar. Your father was an aristocrat. A baron."

"How did you know?"

"I don't know. I feel. You have a joy in you, a singing. It does not come out enough. You must sing that joy of light that is in you. You are magic."

87

Zjennia felt cosy beside him. "You know," he said, "that a thought creates? And Life is a thought. We are living a thought.

"Anyhow I have met your Christian God. You must also know that all is ethereal. With many a million people purporting to worship a god, that god exists, even though it is just ethereal. If all your blood corpuscles got together inside you and elected you as god, and, after all, their life is dependent on you, so they could – then you would become a god. So this ethereal God that religions have created exists ethereally and He said to me that the farce on earth was that His greatest gift was the gift of life and the gift to beget life. Yet all the pretending saints and leaders spent their energies denouncing the libido: denouncing sex, denouncing this spiritual coupling you and I are soon at now. All of them find half their sins in this greatest god-sent gift, 'sex is not for the saints' attitude. And at the best they invent a Mary or a Jesus who they marry in a barren way killing life's life, denouncing lust, and He was thankful animals had not yet invented gods, and He would give saints from all religions a harsh time when He met them face to face. Those religions-mongers also must realise the fact that goods and evils are local figmentations that Czarist rule might be good for Muscovy but evil for Siberia and other countries, that it is bad for society to have a thief, but good for the society of thieves. When we eat a chicken that is good for us but evil for the chicken: when the chicken eats the worm that is good for the chicken but evil for the worm. There is more than that, and it concerns your sister. Her sickness is bad for her, but good for the germ that causes it. Tomorrow I must reach the Fount Home of that germ and persuade it – with no animosity, because it too has a right to live – to leave your sister's body for, as I will explain, she is needed to live longer with us, and more still, it itself will die if she dies. Now what can your religious priests or mullahs do for that? They do not recognise the right of the germ to its existence, so cannot influence it. They cannot reach it, since they have no powers as shamans have, of leaving their bodies and entering other spheres and worlds. The spider, the crawling insect, the sky, the wind, the ice, the tree, the doe, the wolf, thunder and tornado, all have their Life, their Home, and a shaman must know the way to them, while your priests and mullahs behave as if Man alone is of existence.

"We are weak men, we shamans. All of us, and shamanesses too, become what we become, because we were born weaklings and have had a nightmare fight to overcome our own sickness. I was nearly unconscious for three years. So we have developed the weak power of water, and not the tyrant power of mountains, then it ends, as you know, that water cannot conquer mountains."

In a coy burst of frivolity Zjennia asked: "Can you conquer me?"

"Only by letting you conquer me. You are a Goddess of Life among us. I could worship you. Zjennia, have you a husband?"

"I do not know."

"How long since you did not know?"

"Two years."

"Would you feel guilty in breaking a marriage vow this night?"

"He broke his marriage vow to me before he broke my womb!"

"You would feel no guilt?"

"I need you! For God's sake feed my oven!"

88

The procession came down the main street led slowly by the shaman.

Large drums were playing a monotonous beat.

199

They came to the open space before a huge yurt.

The seance would be in the yurt but for now the awaiting crowd were in the compound. A long stretch of smouldering embers began at the street and died off only a few paces from the entrance. By there a large furnace was alive with fire and a ring of rags, tallow and timber sticks were around it.

The drum beat approached. Tulayev, the shaman, frail yet purposeful, had on his regalia and robes of office. An untreated bear skin three-quarters to the ankles, amulets about his chest like a multitude, strips of fox fur let down from a belt, and about that belt marmots' tongues and wolf's teeth and eagles' wings, and symbols for the phallus and the vulva.

The group following were his immediate priests who, for the entire seance would be in attendance. Then came the drummers. They were not the drums of birch and doe-skin Zjennia had been expecting. These were coarse, of wolf skin, and they crescendo-ed louder continuously until all abruptly stopped at the path of the fire.

The priests re-echoed the shaman's words of invocation. The entire community of many hundreds were present.

A priest knelt and removed the boots of the shaman.

The shaman was brought a burning stick with rags of forks of flame. He took a deep breath, bent his head back, plunged the rod down his throat, the flames flew back, then went all but extinct, then the rod was pulled out and all caught sensationally alight again. The priest took the rod and led the leader to the burning embers. Once more a deep breath was taken and the dapper figure of the shaman, to a crescendo of the drums, walked step by slow step the twenty paces to the yurt over the burning embers. The populace watched mesmerised and in disbelief. They gasped and lowered their heads and purred: Mmmmm-nnn-M.

By the entrance two priests held two more rods of fire, one by each door flap, the shaman took one and drank the fire, then the other and drank that too. He was then led to a small tent where he would be anointed and robed for the seance. He took a strangely long drink which, whatever his adherents might think, was pure water.

Inside the yurt, Eva was raised on to a podium. Nikolai, who had refused ever to leave her, was on a stool by her side.

Eva scarcely seemed to be breathing, yet Nikolai knew that a weak pulse was active.

She looked calm, saintly and beautiful, with ebony hair unlike Zjennia's hazel tresses.

The yurt filled with the Tungusi. The centre and the path to the entrances remained empty. Zjennia sat close by. She felt unholy and frightened. She loved Eva.

Nikolai was beyond fear. He had received one message from the shaman. "Believe." That was all. And in blind obedience, almost like a possession, he clung to that and excluded all other emotions.

Eva was absent, 'gone': but she kept her hand in that of her lover's as all else was lost to her.

It was an eternity of time before anything stirred in the silent yurt.

An elder of the commune was squatting on the ground by Zjennia and told her how Tulayev had been impressed by Eva's instinct in returning to the land of her forbears and much of the ritual would follow the practices of the Magyars of a thousand years ago. For instance there was the Taltos pole outside the yurt. 'Taltos' was Hungarian for shaman and a stout pole had been implanted two bodies high, twenty paces from the yurt's entrance.

At long, long last there was a stir and priests entered, bearing pots of tobacco and mushroom. The drummers followed, but now subdued, and now wore small drums fashioned from birch and doe-skin.

Lastly came the shaman resting lightly on the arms of two priests. All did some slow chanting around the podium where the two lovers remained motionless. The entourage circled round three times. Zjennia did not like anything that was happening. "Halala. . . he-he-he. . . halala. . .he-he-he. . ." The dirge went round and round.

The shaman stopped, facing the podium and facing the yurt's entrance. He was about to pass to a trance. A dozen smokes from a dozen pots, some intakings of tobacco and mushroom, more dirging now to a crescendo, a sudden silence almost more thunderous than the preceding noise because of its suddenness, the shaman's eyes rolled backwards, only the whites of his eyes being now seen, he was unsteady and had to be supported by two immediate priests. He passed to a trance.

Zjennia was frightened. The shaman's enormous eyes had become white ice. Horrific. Where could she run? But it was for Eva. Yet this was insane.

The Hungarian Taltos pole was outside in the compound. When a bird alighted on it, the shaman would enter the soul of the bird and fly off. He would fly to the end of the world.

Alarmingly quickly the shaman shouted "Now!" The yurt flaps were flung open, the pole was there, and there to the all-but-disbelief of all Tungusi present, a bird had alighted on it and could be seen in the flickers of fire flames. No one knew what bird it was. The two priests helped the shaman as he lay prone on the ground and then said "He has left us."

The bird flew away.

All Zjennia's horrors were becoming petrified into a trance of her own.

202

"He is passing over the Yenesei," the priest by the prone shaman was saying. "A great scent is there and is being brought towards the Volga by the west wind. Massive herds of reindeer are following the scent and migrating. They will reach here in four weeks and it will be a fine hunting season."

A hum of great approval passed from one to another among the assembly.

"Both the Bokkobushka and the Mindui will have children this summer," was the next remark, baffling Zjennia who stifled an idiotic laugh. "I must hurry on," came in a hushed whisper from the ground where the shell of the shaman lay. Even the sceptic Zjennia saw indeed that the shaman seemed out of his body.

"It's so far to the end of the earth," came from the ground.

After a long silence these words came: "I do not want to, but I have to change to the Sky-God Horse. The air is so heavy, the Sky-God Bird can no longer fly with the weight of my soul depressing it. I turn the Sky-God Bird into a flint-lock and put it in my pocket and continue on the Sky-God Horse to the outermost limits of the earth."

Soon: "I have reached there, but there is an impassable swamp. It is lucky I retained the Bird. I've changed my flint-lock back to the Bird and fly over the swamp. The cuckoo awaits us at the earth's last swamp."

Zjennia knew what was happening to her. She was passing out of reality into unreality and these Tungusi all around her knew unreality and believed in it, so that for them, they were merely living it. Zjennia let herself be sucked into it also, then swept on with it.

"This swamp is immeasurably long but we are coming now to the centre. In the centre is a golden aspen with silver leaves. It is the Tree of Life. At the bottom of it is the Water of Life. On the top of it sits the cuckoo.

The cuckoo helps anyone who reaches him. I tell how I need some Water of Life, because back in north Samara lies someone whose Water of Life is all but spent. The Sky God and I are given some and we must return. The cuckoo noted I wore the Bear's Skin therefore he knew which Water of Life to give. People of the Por regard the bear as their own. Some call it The Old Man of the Hill. Others call it Grandfather's Claws. A female bear gave birth to the first Por woman and the first Por woman gave birth to the first Hungarian shaman. Wait for me, O my people, I will return."

There was a stirring among the crowd, such as one might experience in between items at a concert. But soon all were settled and awaited the return of their shaman.

There was another long spell and people began again the refrain "Mmmmm-nnn-mm. Mmmmm-nnn-mm."

At last there was a light stirring by the body on the ground. "Give a little," it said. And there was a small pot. A priest took it and held it to the lips of Eva. She could scarcely open her lips to take any liquid, and was all but unconscious, but some drops did flow in.

"I must rest a short while," said the prostrate form. But soon it said, all but inaudibly: "I had first to bring Life. It had all but ended here. Now I must seek out the sickness. I will go now."

The eyes, which for some moments had been human, returned to the ice white again.

The Mmmmm-nnn-mm went on, and though Zjennia may one day reach a hundred, she will never be able to forget that yurt, those Tungusi at the squat, and that incantation, on and on and on and on.

"It's in the great underground, in the underworld." Much that the prostrate form was mumbling, the priest repeated in louder voice and could just be heard above the never-ending incantations.

204

"I have at last reached the Womb and the Source and the Crucible of the sickness. I had difficulty in passing the house of the parents," he said. 'Our parents are dead!' murmured Zjennia to herself. "There was a gruff servant at the gate entrance who said no one must pass," the voice from the ground continued. "I knew what I had to do. I brushed right past, and past the parents too. I had to. I had to brush through and on. Then below all earth I explained at the Crucible of the Sickness that One of Them infests Eva's body and is fast using it all up. It is probably frightened of how it shall survive should it leave her shelter. But her life is wanted as part of the Plan of Life and she shall live! The Source told me the key to speak directly to It in the body and I must explain directly. The Source said it would send help for It to return to them and live on at the Source."

The breathing was lessening in the prostrate form of the shaman. It was a shell, but the shell was taking over and the body might end as a corpse.

"I have to do it. I have to do it," said the form.

There was a shudder of fear throughout the assembly as the priest repeated the words, showing his own fear in his own voice. "Pray for our leader," said the priest.

All burst loudly into "Mmmmm-nnn-mm". Then dozens took over.

"Tell Nikolai to be brave."

The priest told Nikolai to be brave. He told Nikolai, and Zjennia just heard, that It had refused to leave Eva: that the shaman was taking out Eva's soul and sending it to the roof of the yurt. This way Eva had her own concentration on her own soul and the way was cleared for the shaman to pass right through to It. He would tell It that there would be no more life to feed on if It did not leave as Eva would only return to her form if It left.

Nikolai, in tears that did everything but kill him,

clutched Eva's hand tightly, but felt an awful coldness as her soul left for the roof.

Zjennia felt insane, but was mesmerised and, though she tried, she could not stir.

The whole concourse knew that this was the moment of nightmare.

There was a great shaking in the prostrate form on the floor.

"Raise me up."

Two priests raised the 'absent' form. It began to walk around the podium, on the arms, as crutches, of his men. All priests followed solemnly. The drums took up "Halala-he-he-he Halala-he-he-he." The Tungusi dirged "Mmmmm-nnn-mm". Everything got louder. All Unreality was there.

"It has agreed to leave and we must catch it."

"It has agreed to leave and we must catch it!" cried the priest.

"It has agreed to leave and we must catch it!!!" cried the multitude.

Heaven stirred.

The bowl that held the little Water of Life was in the hands of the shaman supported by the priests, while more priests supported the shaman himself at the elbows.

Round and round and round. Round they went, the whole group around the lovers.

"It is near the mouth and must be caught. Now!!"

Like a crazed automaton the shell of the shaman dashed at Eva, placed the bowl under the lips: "I have It! I have It!"

"He has It! He has It!" from the priest.

"Our leader has It!! He has It!!" from the squatting multitude.

In a scurrying, jolting scuffle the priests hurried their leader to the entrance, the flaps were flung open, the shaman lurched forward, emptied furiously the bowl into the night with a throwing movement. There was a light as of a fire-fly on the Taltos pole, then in the trees, then deeper in the woods, then as a pin-prick in the gloom beyond.

Talayev had collapsed, as dead, the bowl beside him.

Zjennia could see no breathing in Eva.

And when they carried the shaman back, she could see no breathing in his form either.

The mesmeric trance was still upon her.

Nikolai still held Eva's hand. But it was too cold and he knew all was gone. And he had no life to live for.

There they lay, two prostrate bodies: Eva and the shaman.

The concourse was silent.

How long they stayed there. . . what indeed is time? the silence, the sitting.

Some got up and left.

In the end, most were gone.

At last Zjennia shook in her cocoon and went to Nikolai. His eyes were all hurt and tears were waiting behind the hurt.

Still he held Eva's hand.

Tulayev was as dead as well. The priests said "We cannot tell. It may be one day. It may be three days. It may be our Tulayev has left us. We will sit."

After – an aeon of time? – the smallest tremor came to Eva. Nikolai cried out "Eva lives!"

Zjennia quickly felt her sister's pulse. And felt nothing. Had she seen the tremor too? "This goblet is of gold," she uttered, seeing the bowl of the Water of Life.

Another aeon of time elapsed. Another tremor! "She lives!"

Zjennia said to a priest "What liquid have you?"

"I will fetch some." And he left. And returned with some mare's milk. "Only moisten her lips," he said.

This, lover and sister did. And then they stared at their dear Eva and awaited a miracle.

And the miracle came.

A whole movement! The ebony tresses moved from one side to the other. It has happened!

"When the shaman first gave Eva the Water of Life I felt a warmth go in her. Oh, Zjennia!"

But there was no miracle for the shaman.

The priests merely repeated. "Perhaps one day, perhaps three. Perhaps none. We will not know. Because he has not been in the world all evening, all night. He may not find the road back. He is in a death-sleep."

And so it stayed till the cocks crew. One, just about alive; one, just about dead.

89

Two days later Zjennia entered the house of Tulayev the shaman.

His eyes were open. There was no movement in his body. But the priests knew he had returned to them.

"You saved the life of my sister," Zjennia said.

The shaman answered in a feeble voice: "Nikolai's belief saved her. Believe in belief."

He turned his head away.

She impulsively fell at his feet. She wanted to stay with him. Forever.

With his head still turned from her he said: "As I flew over the Yenesei returning, I saw a boon for you. A boon was coming this way. Two days after you have returned to Ch——, go to the outskirts and wait."

She only wanted to stay with *him*! And be with *him* always.

Still with his face turned away, he added: "My love for you is wound up. I have wound it into a silver ball and you cannot come back to me for it, for it is out of me and travels on with you forever wherever you go. You have enjoyed sex with a priestly puppy, with a lecherous hippopotamus, with a boy and a butcher, with an aesthetic shaman. But a bull is your boon: and he is coming back to you and has crossed the Yenesei."

90

They were many weeks outside Omsk when Boris cut a reed and carved a flute and played Stanka Razin.

"Why haven't we had more music from you, Boris?"

"I had a black load inside me which crushed my breast and hammered my head. When you got me my pardon that went. I'm on my way to Samara and I am free again."

"Free," mused Sergei, playing with their fire with a stick. "A sort of freedom. Back to Samara and back to society, back to conventions and laws. I'll tell you a funny contradiction: I heard a mistress tell it to her lover: 'You will live free, forever. Under my yoke.' That should be written. as the maxim of every Czar, government, Patriarch, Pope, Mullah, Elder, Shaman, every religion ever invented, every society be it secret, open, feudalistic, Cossack, Capitalist or Napoleonic. . . many husbands issue the edict to their wives, many wives issue it to their husbands, and, as I began, a mistress issued it to her lover 'You will live free forever. Under my yoke.' I hope your yoke will be sweet in Samara. But, free? You and I won't know more freedom than being here, you and I, Poogavitsa and Kukurooza, a fire of aspen, a flute of hollow reed. Give us a song of the Volga River."

Boris and Sergei were only a few days from the fork in the road where Sergei would ride north west to Moscow and Boris south west to Samara.

A sudden upheaval all around and the two realised they were being attacked. Horses appeared from a dozen spots behind them.

"Don't wait for me," shouted Boris. "Gallop on! God speed!"

Sergei wouldn't. Poogavitsa rose to its best, but it was no gallop.

Each man carried furs and skins with them. "I'll head them a little to the right," yelled Sergei. "I'll drop some loot. Don't you. Not yet. The loot will pull them my way. Hurry on!"

And he had reined away and was already dropping a few skins. The horsemen dashed down upon like locusts.

"It's Steltzi and gang!" yelled Boris.

"I know!" Sergei yelled back.

Yes, the loot slowed them down: there was fighting for the skins. But Streltzi and Yakov and ten others came back on the pursuit.

Sergei dropped more. And Poogavitsa was gaining fine ground.

Sergei won them a respite, then crossed back to Boris. "I have no more. Give me yours."

Boris handed across his load, and Sergei tried the trick again. "Dear Zjennia, forgive me! They were for you!" The loss stung Boris deeply. "But my own skin for you first, Zjennia!"

210

It was like throwing carcasses down to wolves. The pack closed round them. Fought. Then continued the chase again.

The pair had gained more ground and Sergei returned and was riding with Boris.

Then the terrible thing happened.

They entered a wood: a split in the path, Sergei went one way, Boris the other.

What could they do?

Each knew he must ride on.

They lost each other.

No clearing showed the other anywhere.

The pack behind split too.

Boris was becoming petrified. He cried out three times to Zjennia, three times to God, three times to Samara, then once more a cry which rent the sky to Zjennia.

The plain again. A stream! Oh God, no! Poogavitsa went off course across the wasteland. Boris did nothing. The stream was upon them. A dip in the road. Poogavitsa charged down. Boris still did nothing. A landing-stage was there! The horse dashed on to it, leapt, fell in the water, Boris clung on, one, two stumbles only, the horse was up, out of the water, and away with the wind. Boris said "Poogavitsa, in Samara I will build a stable of gold and you will be in it."

The following pack were defeated, reaching the stream at different points. And they rode up and down by the stream. Then one or two ventured into it. And at least six got across in the end. And because it was an open steppe, they could hunt their prey yet.

A terrible time went. But the pack closed.

And on the gaping open land, two on the flanks were ahead of Boris, and four behind gained until they were breathing on him.

A horse reared and fell. Exhausted. Two others

211

slowed. But Streltzi on one flank and a second Cossack on the other side, closed in. Poogavitsa ran and ran and ran.

And step by step he gained. The Cossack steeds could give no more. Pace by pace, three paces by three paces, ten paces by ten paces the miracle Orlov steed gained. 'It was as if Zjennia was pulling on a magic string and pulling us home to her.'

When Steltzi stopped he took up his gun and fired. And missed. And fired. And missed.

The little horse didn't slow down its pace. Just running on and on.

All that noon. And half that night.

91

They reached a small town. Boris unharnessed his horse, walked a few paces around, then returned.

"Poogavitsa, you might not understand but I have to talk to someone, so I'll talk to you. I have to take Zjennia home a fur and a jewel, otherwise I cannot go home at all. I have an incredibly magnificent sable sewn in my schuba. I have a fine little emerald in a neat gold and enamel casket. That's all I have. The rest we threw to those Cossack wolves. Zjennia lives in Ch——, in the Samara region, and that's where we are going and that's where I am going to build you a stable of pure gold. Now I forgot to tell you that Sergei and I did not mean to separate when we did and he went off with all our money and almost all our ammunition. So what have we to sell? My schuba. But if I sell my schuba I disclose my sable, and half of Russia, no, well nigh all of it, would kill me for that sable, it is such a miracle, so I cannot sell my schuba. There is the sable and the jewel, but if I sell either of them I can never show my face at home. Do you know you have not changed your expression all the time I have been talking to you, you've just looked down. Why do you only look down? Now if I do not buy you oats, I also will not get home. So what can I do? What did you say? Did you say 'split it'?"

A passer-by, thinking this long dissertation with the little horse was of a deranged man, had said: "Split it. Break it up, man," and then had walked on.

Boris looked at the passer-by, then back to Poogavitsa: "He's right," he said. And Boris left for the Bank.

The Bank Manager received him and heard an old familiar story of a traveller being robbed by brodyagi. Then Boris took out the jewel, explained he must keep the jewel but would sell the gold and enamel casket, how much for the casket.

The Bank Manager called in his boy, asked him to take the little casket to Smernov's the only precious stone assessor in town and ask for three prices: one for the emerald, one for the fitting the emerald was set in, and one for the whole casket.

Boris said: "No. What price the casket. Only that."

The manager sighed, dismissed the boy, and the two men talked of other things. The boy returned with the news that the casket had no gold in it. Only gold plating, and the value was fifty roubles.

Boris bit his lip, but said: "Then, sir, there is your price. Now pawn me that and I will leave it with you and will be back for it."

The manager was used to strange business, and this was strange business, but offered a pawn ticket and Boris took the money.

He bought the richest oats, fed himself greatly also,

treated himself to a small brick of tea and rode out before dark.

Both should have rested well that night except that Boris had lost his zest for Samara. He could not face Zjennia without gifts! He had saved well and worked well, and had bought the proud prizes. Cossack wolves! All the bitterness for Alexis, the priest mounted inside him again. He was to blame for this entire nightmare. He knew Boris's character. Boris hated such a stupid convention of whips in one boot and jewels in another. He would give Zjennia all the furs, skins, jewels in Muscovy, but from love and lust, not because of a child's party game! Alexis had known that! He could have released him from the room to have slipped a jewel into the second boot. The damn insipid twit of a nit of a priest.

So Boris only slept between bursts of anger.

92

Three days they travelled together. Boris was distraught at his losses, wondered where Sergei was, but felt the magnet of Zjennia pulling, pulling.

They were, in retrospect, three happy days.

Love consumed him. He felt one tenth Boris and nine tenths Zjennia. That marshmallow voice. Those hazel eyes. The body of a serpent inside a woman, Sergei had said, though when and why Boris could not recall. "Gods are in heaven and are easy to handle. Goddesses are on earth, and men cannot forget it."

And Boris didn't mind how much he was going to get

consumed. Zjennia consuming him would make him complete.

Three happy days. A few streams. A road like a path. Copses of birches which Boris had been 'sent to Siberia to count and was returning having missed out on one or two.' A rare osprey. Many a quail. Wag-tails, reeds and steppe-land. The road getting sandier leading to a small desert. Sun beating down.

A little horse. A tall lone rider.

93

When Boris opened his eyes next morning Poogavitsa was not standing up. He always slept standing.

Boris, hollowed out inside utterly, went to him.

Poogavitsa was dead.

Boris, hollowed out inside utterly. . .

94

"Oh dear God, close your eyes!" Boris raised his head to heaven.

"If I don't reach Zjennia, nothing has any meaning! Don't let the angels see!"

And he plunged his knife into the little horse and ripped off strips of carcase for food.

"Zjennia, a madman is coming to you. Send me your

strength. The gods cannot bear me any more. I have only you."

He gathered his tiny bundle and started the trek of a deranged man.

In the little desert he was overcome with thirst and, ill, could not proceed. He took off his schuba, and with his knife marked out a circle in the sand. Then he hollowed it out till the space was the shape of a shallow bowl – a stride wide. Then he placed his drinking mug in the bottom of the bowl. Then he took off his shirt, then with tiny stones pinned the shirt down around the perimeter, tight, so that it was taut across. Then he dropped the biggest pebble he could find, though small it was, exactly in the circle above his mug. Then left for the rough shelter from the sun of his schuba laid across some shrub. After minutes only he returned, and the heat on the shirt had sucked up its first drops of water from the desert, and they had slid down the sloping shirt till he had counted seven drops fall into the mug; seven for the letters of Zjennia, for if there was any life-line left it was only her: he would reach Samara on her pull alone or he would perish. Yes, Z,J,E,N,N,I,A, he had counted them drop then returned to his shield from the sun.

He tried to control himself but could not. When the drinking vessel was half full only he took it out and drained it. The tiny relief was real and he placed the vessel back. But dare not delay more than the once filling of it. Also the water in each desert 'hand-made bowl' was tiny and every fill-up would lessen the amount there to be sucked up. He should try another spot. But he must not stop.

An unbearable time elapsed, the mug was full, he took it out so carefully, sipped, then began to drain it, but knew what he had to do: he had to let Zjennia do the shouting 'Stop Boris!!' Then add: 'I forbid you to drain the last drops!'

216

He knew the strength of this. If he, his mind, knew he carried water, however tiny the quantity, it was an ocean of relief. If he drained that, an insanity of thirst could seize him. 'I swear to you Zjennia, I will not drink this little last, until I know where there is more!'

He went on. How he would have liked to have been shot of his schuba! The weight of it! But in its lining was its sable, in its pocket was its emerald. Without them, Boris would lay down and die. But where was his gun? Somehow, somewhere he had lost his gun. He could not think where. At the water stop? No. When? All was blank.

And on and on he trudged.

The desert was crossed. Sweet steppe-land appeared again.

If he found water, he would sleep. He had food yet: if he could awake to food and water, yes, he would sleep.

He found a little bubbling stream. The noise it made! Uncanny.

95

Days went. He would have been home now if with Poogavitsa.

He checked the thought. He must not think of his horse. Nor of Sergei. Nor of anything. Zjennia, only her.

Days went and food went.

He lost all senses except a sense of direction and a sense of purpose. He knew he was on the right track. There was no other way.

Had he passed huts? Farms? He had not realised any. Yet surely he should have done? He began to feel landmarks. Hopes grew. Yet, a farm, why had he passed no farm?

Fact was, he scarcely raised his eyes off the road. He just blindly allowed the step behind to force the step in front. He had kept that little water in his drinking vessel by tying over it a rip off his shirt and by keeping it at his waist always upright. He had not felt Zjennia release him from his promise yet: there must always be a little there. Food now, not water, was the urgency. But that vessel gave a touch of power: Boris carried three things now, not two, for Zjennia: a sable, an emerald, and a water of life.

96

Food went. More days went. It was not Boris any more. A bent trudging form, in one direction with one purpose, occasionally looking up, screwing his eyes directly to the skyline in front, then trudging more.

How many days.

No food.

Just trudging.

There was no more than the shade of Boris left. He had all but lost the purpose but not the direction. Zjennia was becoming a veil and not flesh and blood. All he really knew was that he must keep straight on.

He did not drop. Just once: it was a faint: he fell where he was: for all he knew it was hours: he awoke and trudged on. If stumbling in a dream is trudging. That was only once.

He could not see, but he felt there was something on

218

the horizon. Nothing was three-dimensional. He felt like a shadow and he felt he saw a veil, a grey veil of a steeple? was it?

Nothing registered. And he just had sufficient consciousness to know he could at any moment start seeing a mirage. A church? He looked up again. Screwed his eyes. Probably not. Just perhaps. It was not. It was a cloud trick.

On he trudged.

Was that?. . . Was that?. . . . He was failing. Was that?.. . . He had no more to him. Sorry, Zj. . . Was that? Oh, how he had wanted to return proud and resplendent with gifts and glory! This is not worth a return, not like this. How can I face her? Zjennia!

Miles more. This is the road that goes round the world and stays where it is. 'All roads lead to Moscow,' the saying is. 'All roads lead to Zjennia,' said Boris. One more, just one more effort.

He looked up. He stopped. But immediately continued because he knew that if he really stopped he would not start going again.

He remembers a silly something happened then. 'You can finish the water now,' he heard. He fumbled for it. But would not touch it.

A grey silhouette was before him. A figure. The fence around Ch——. He drank the water. The last drops.

He went on.

The silhouette was a form. It was coming to him. Oh come! come!

They met! Zjennia and Boris!

"Tell me only, is it you? Is it you Zjennia?"

"Boris. It is me!"

"I have only one sable and one emerald."

"What are you talking about. Boris, beloved one, lie quietly here. I will hurry to get help."

She kissed him.

97

Zjennia told Boris: "Boris, you have to go. The call-up papers have come for you to join the Army. You are to go the moment you have strength, out this back way. Alexis, the priest, will meet you at the edge of the wood. He will ride with you to a hiding place we have found many miles from here and you must hide there until this call-up is over. No one in the town knows that you have come home except Alexis and he has sworn not to betray us."

Boris was set to leave. He stood at dawn, beside a new horse, with a gun, fine ammunition, and the assurance that all he could immediately wish for was at the cottage.

But he did not mount the horse.

"Boris! For God's sake be off! I cannot stand it if they catch you now!!"

Still Boris remained rooted where he was.

He stared at the east and not at the north which was the way he was to go.

"Boris!! Do you want me to be insane?"

Some soldiers appeared.

"Boris!! I'll go mad if you don't go!!"

"They are not soldiers," said Boris.

Zjennia held her head in terror.

A riff-raff crowd came up on horseback. And Boris was right, for he had recognised one of them.

The leader spoke.

The man Boris had recognised came forward: "I know this man," he said.

It was Viktor of the Mail Coach robbery. He edged forward to be at the side of the leader.

"How do you know him?"

"He saved my life."

"Then tell him our demands."

Viktor said: "We need water, fodder for our horses, one meal, and then we will leave your town unharmed. Tell us the name and place of the Head Man of this town."

"This is all right," said Boris to Zjennia. "Please tell him."

Zjennia, shaken still, told what was asked.

They were about to leave when the leader asked: "How did he save your life, Anatoly?"

Viktor, alias Lavrenti, now Anatoly said: "I was being attacked by a bear. This friend, of all strange things, stunned the bear with the butt of his rifle on his nose. Then he shot him."

"Then he knew his bears. That's the only place you can stun a bear. Should we take your friend with us?"

"I can't advise it," said Viktor. "He has leprosy."

"Oh."

And they moved away. Viktor delayed behind.

"Are you a revolutionary?" asked Boris.

"I'm not sure. I haven't found out what I'm supposed to be yet. I thought I was a Nihilist but it now seems I'm not. But it's as nice a way of getting to the Capital as any. They picked me up like they nearly picked you up."

"Thanks for the leprosy," said Boris.

"Yes, I hadn't thought of that then. I said I had a weak heart but the Decembrists or the Nihilists or whatever we are didn't let that bother them."

"What about the call-up for the Czar's Army?" asked Boris with his hand on Zjennia's arm.

"The war is over, didn't you know? all call-ups are cancelled, didn't you know?"

221

"No! Sergei and I only got our pardons a few weeks ago."

"Up your ass with your pardon! The Czar sent you to Siberia, didn't he? Any enemy of the Czar is a made man now! But hang on to your leprosy. That might come in useful."

And gangleshanks Viktor rode off.

"Zjennia!" cried Boris in a near falsetto voice. "How many children did you say you must have?"

"Six, Boris, six! Not one less!"

AFTERWORD

The Czar had fallen. It was an event of gigantic significance, yet neither Boris, nor Viktor could understand it. Nor could anyone else from the Ukraine to Irkutsk and beyond.

A notice about the Abdication was posted on the wall of the big grain storage building in Samara. It said that Russia was to be a Republic. People stood around it shaking heads.

"So we are to be a Republic" said the blacksmith. "Why not? As long as we have a good Czar at the head."

Next Sunday they all gathered in the church of Vosknesenie. Zjennia wore a red cockade in her hair. She had been looking at herself in the mirror. The needle of fire in her eyes was burning brightly. Alexis, the priest, was at the altar. He did not dare look at Zjennia. He could feel molten lava in his veins.

Zjennia walked out of the church. . . Her head was high. She clung to Boris. His arm was tightly wound round her waist.

222

One of the elders heard a rumour that there wouldn't be any churches or priests in the new Russia. "Alexis will have to enlist in the Army" they all laughed.

"I will find you a horse like Poogavitsa" said Boris. Alexis hung his head. He was frightened.

"The Czar has gone," said the boatman, spitting sunflower seeds into the water. "So what? Everything is going to be the same as before!"

He was wrong. Everything was to be different from now on. Three hundred and four years had gone by since a sixteen-year-old Romanov boy had ascended the throne of All Russias. And now his descendent had given the Crown back to the people. The Russian Armies had withdrawn from the war. Boris will not have to worry about the call-up any more.

In faraway Petrograd Sergei had joined the Revolution. They had just stormed the Winter Palace. . . sporting red armbands and cockades the mobs were to march on Tsarskoe Selo. They had all become rich from the looting. . . they were awash in oceans of vodka. "Death to the Czar! Death to the Empress!" they chanted. Sergei hoped to become a Commissar. He was now a hero of the Revolution; his years in Siberia were paying off.

Boris and Zjennia were walking along the river to Samara arm in arm. It was autumn. Zjennia was now heavily pregnant; she moved slowly. Many changes had come to the village. Alexis had gone and the local church had been closed. There were rumours that the Czar was being held in a prison in Siberia.

Boris felt a sense of loss. He could not understand why he felt it. Strangely it had something to do with the Czar.

"You know," he said to Zjennia. "The Czar sent me to

jail, that is true. But still he was our Czar. Now they have put him away and we have none."

"Shut up Boris!" said Zjennia. "Don't talk like this. For your son it will be like a new dawn on the Volga; he will be born a free man. God willing."

Zjennia crossed herself furtively. They walked on.